POP
SALVATION

LANCE REYNALD

POP SALVATION

A NOVEL

HARPER PERENNIAL

NEW YORK • LONDON • TORONTO • SYDNEY • NEW DELHI • AUCKLAND

HARPER ● PERENNIAL

HarperCollins books may be purchased for educational, business, or sales
promotional use. For information please write: Special Markets Department,
HarperCollins Publishers, 10 East 53rd Street, New York, NY 10022.

FIRST EDITION

Designed by Aline C. Pace

Library of Congress Cataloging-in-Publication Data
Reynald, Lance.
      Pop salvation : a novel / Lance Reynald.—1st ed.
         p. cm.
    ISBN 978-0-06-167297-2
      1. Alienation (Social psychology)—Fiction. 2. Pop art—Influ-
ence—Fiction. 3. Washington (D.C.)—Fiction. I. Title.
PS3618.E955P67 2009
813'.6—dc22
                    2008039150

09 10 11 12 13 OV/RRD 10 9 8 7 6 5 4 3 2 1

for A

There is one thing I must tell you because I just found it to be a truth. . . . You must always be yourself no matter what the price. It is the highest form of morality.

Candy Darling

Persons, places, and events have inspired this story and
may cause it to resemble the truth,

though the telling is fiction . . .
except for Andy Warhol, he was his own masterpiece . . .
. . . and *The Rocky Horror Picture Show* is an institution.

Come with me.

philosophy (life): from A to me

Everyone could use a philosophy.

Religion is supposed to be a kind of philosophy. I don't think I buy it, but I like the art. You have to give them credit there. All those religious paintings really are amazing. Great paintings that come out of all those sad stories you hear in Sunday school. Beautiful monotony born out of someone's outdated philosophy. They're all the same, those paintings.

Andy Warhol had his own philosophy: *From A to B and back again.* Andy was a celebrity, maybe even the most famous celebrity ever. It was all from living his philosophy.

Everyone can use a philosophy.

It pulls you through.

It might even make you a celebrity.

Once you become that kind of celebrity everything else about you falls away. You don't have to worry about your past and the things that happened. You have a better life and if you're a big enough celebrity no one can touch you. All your friends will be great celebrities and no one will even care what came before.

It's finding your way to that kind of celebrity that is the trick. Having a good philosophy can really help you get through.

Andy Warhol started his life as a sickly, effeminate, Czech boy in Pittsburgh.

He died a legend.

The right philosophy gets you there.

I don't know how I made it through life before I learned all of that, but once I did, I tried to never forget it.

learning (childhood)

Seen and not heard.

The golden rule of my childhood.

A great deal of effort and conversation was put into how I was seen, how I should be heard. In 1983 I'd spent most of my summer break on my father's sailboat. I started at Capital Day School with a summer's long sunburn. I just don't tan. The sunblock separated and didn't spread very well through the last few trips out on the boat, so my end-of-summer burn looked like tiger stripes in various shades of pink and red.

Most of the kids in my new school thought this was pretty funny.

But it really wasn't that funny.

At the day school I got the seen part all wrong from the beginning. I had been tested at the beginning of the summer. It was decided that I should start my new school by skipping a grade. This made me smaller and younger than the rest of my class. I was never a sixth grader; a skipped year made me different from my peers from that point on.

The heard part didn't go right either. I spent the first eleven years of my life in Texas. I couldn't lose my Southern accent. I used words like *fixin'*.

Always fixin' to do something.

The other kids thought *fixin'* was pretty funny, too. They laughed at me whenever I said it, then they called me a hick. I tried so hard to be like everyone else, with their accents that sounded like they were from nowhere. I got tired from trying so hard and ended up back with the *fixin'*s and the *y'all*s. The kids laughed, and again I was a hick.

If I hadn't spent my first six years of school in Lubbock, Texas, I wouldn't have been fixin'. I would have sounded like them. I might have stood a chance of having some friends and not being known as the hick. But a few simple words and a slower cadence to my voice left me friendless.

I hated my new school, but we were not moving back to Texas. My dad and his new wife made that perfectly clear. My new life was in Washington, D.C. If it took the best schools, tutors, and hell freezing over I would be broken of my *fixin'*s and *y'all*s.

Fixin' means "about to." I was about to become like the other kids. At least that was what my dad wanted. What he always seemed to want from me.

I thought I was hopeless. I didn't know how to be like them.

I didn't think anyone could ever change themselves that much.

To become something else, someone else.

To reimagine, reinvent, reemerge.

I thought I'd never be able to be anything else.

Always on the outside, never belonging.

Mrs. Spaulding talked nice.

Excuse me, she was well spoken.

Mrs. Spaulding was my English teacher at the day school, and she would come to our house to tutor me on Tuesday and Thursday afternoons. She talked—spoke—like she might have been from England. Not the same part of England as my nanny, Tracy, but a smarter part of England. Mrs. Spaulding said it wasn't England at all when I asked her. She said it was enunciation. We worked on enunciation on Tuesday and Thursday afternoons.

I would pronounce my vocabulary words out loud. Then, after sighing and pushing her gray-streaked, bobbed hair behind her ears, she would point out the parts of the words I wasn't saying right. It felt like she was trying to teach me a new language altogether. Enunciation was hard work, but she never lost her patience with me. She sat next to me with her hands folded in her lap as I struggled through our lessons. Everything about me was unrefined in contrast to her East Coast perfection of twinsets and pearls. She had style and grace, that much I knew. Right down to the red Volvo she drove home to Foxhall Road, she seemed perfect to me. Just like the pictures of Jacqueline Kennedy in the American history museum. I wanted to learn how to fit in like that.

Even with a little enunciation the kids at school still called me a hick, or would that be an hick? The *h* still trips me up. It's what I was back then, so I should know what to do with the *h*.

I didn't like spending recess with the other kids laughing at me, so Mrs. Spaulding would let me sit in her classroom while she ate lunch. Sometimes we would use this time to practice my enunciation, sounding out the syllables of words, trying to smooth out my accent.

No more *fixin'*. More *about to*.

When we were not working on my accent, we would sit and read. Silent together, with our lunches and our books. The day school gave us some tough books to read and Mrs. Spaulding tried to help me understand them better. They were hard to understand but I enjoyed reading them. We had finished *The Phantom Tollbooth* and had started *Lord of the Flies*. Mrs. Spaulding said it was the symbolism that made *Tollbooth* funny. She tried to explain the symbolism to me, but it's in the vocabulary. I thought if I could learn some more of the words it would be even more funny. A strange book.

Lord of the Flies had lots of symbolism, too. I wasn't sure I understood it all. I just know I felt a lot like Simon. The other kids on the island didn't like him. I wondered if they would like him in the day school? I really don't think those kids would've liked him any more than they liked me. I was pretty sure I'd end up like Simon if it was left to the other kids in the day school to decide. I hadn't seen them sharpening sticks at recess or anything, but the thought had probably crossed a few minds.

Sometimes we would just eat our lunch.

Even Mrs. Spaulding's lunch seemed smarter than mine. Half an apple, cottage cheese with black pepper on top. She would take her time eating, as though she rewarded herself with one bite for every page she read. I would keep my eyes on my book so we didn't have to talk about our food. My lunches were just another thing in my life that were different. I had enough hassles without drawing attention to my lunch.

I got peanut butter sandwiches our housekeeper made special for me every morning. The bread flattened with a rolling pin and the crusts cut off. Then the peanut butter and grape jelly rolled up like roll cakes. Two rolls of peanut butter and jelly in a Baggie, just the way I liked them. They looked special, different from the other lunches. I tried not to eat them in front of the other kids.

Someone would laugh at me.

They were just sandwiches.

I hated it there.

Even with enunciation and hard books, I wanted to die.

Enunciation lessons were expanding my vocabulary, so now words would occasionally get me into trouble.

Being seen *and* heard was leading to more problems.

One afternoon James Marshall decided to rip the alligator off my shirt. I had been seen.

It wasn't my first problem with James Marshall. Of all the kids at the school, he hated me the most. James wanted to make sure I always knew I was different and not welcome. I was the enemy, the weak one. No one challenged James on it. James took great delight in making certain that everyone saw all of my flaws. Nothing went undetected. The alligator didn't have to come off my shirt to prove I didn't belong. It was obvious in everything about me. I was smaller than the other kids, I had an accent, my stepmother dressed me in a preppy style, all my school clothes were shiny and new, and even my hair was combed neatly into place and sprayed every morning. I was more effeminate than the other boys, and even some of the girls. And the other kids had been together since kindergarten. All of these things were known to me and everyone else. No, the alligator came off my shirt to remind me that I was different and would never have friends in my new school. It was another way to keep me in my place and get a few laughs. Beyond that, I'm guessing the alligator was sacrificed to little more than spite.

Yet I'm the one whose parents were called to pick me up.

Not so much for an alligator-shirt emergency. Certainly one can live with an alligator-free shirt.

It was a matter of word choices.

"You bastard."

James Marshall is a bastard, but that can go a few different ways:

A natural response to having one's alligator removed.

An insult.

A statement of fact.

I had no idea that it was a fact when I first said it, but my father became aware of the fact when he discussed the matter with Principal Montgomery.

No matter how you looked at it James Marshall was a bastard. He was the ringleader in terrorizing me at the day school. Everything about me was scrutinized. Every difference was fair game in his bully tool kit. If the mildest Southern draw tinged a single word, or if I wore a pink shirt, double-knotted my shoelaces, swayed my hips too much, or did any-thing unique in any way, James noticed. He would make sure to point out any distinct flaws to the rest of the kids. Anything could be a reason to ridicule me. Once something was found I'd get grief for it for the next week or so. Then it would start again when James found another flaw. He always found some-thing to chastise me for. The bastard behaved like a bastard. A title earned in action and on paper.

Yet I wasn't allowed to remind him of this fact, no matter what he did to me.

Still, every day James managed to remind me that I would never be like the others, never be one of them, and never be accepted. I talked wrong, dressed wrong, walked the wrong way, and came from the wrong place.

I still wanted to die.

To go the way of my alligator.

learning (art)

During the last week of my seventh grade school year, the faculty tried to keep us busy without having actual assignments due. This meant we would walk or take the Metro to the museums on the Mall. I'd already seen the Air and Space, Natural History and American History museums. These were the places my stepmother would have my nanny take me when there was nothing left to do at home and she was tired of talking to me. But I'd never seen the art galleries until the end of the year field trips.

The National Gallery of Art, the East Wing, and the Hirsh horn Museum and Sculpture Garden: an artistic triangle. We were free to wander the galleries at our own pace for a few hours, under strict orders from Principal Montgomery to behave ourselves or have our grades for the year voided. The classic art of the National Gallery was just too much to take in, most of it dark and morbid. Sad portraits and religious art housed in a domed marble palace.

It was an underground conveyor that carried me under Fourth Street to the East Wing. Everything transitioned as I moved from the classical world past the water-wall fountain via a mirrored tube that housed a moving sidewalk and disembarked at the concourse level of the I. M. Pei building.

The National Gallery's modern collections.

In front of me four white plaster girls danced a circle under the mobile suspended from the immense skylight window. I had never seen a building so full of light. Most buildings in Washington, D.C., are caverns of cold marble hallways with dim lights. Buildings in the style of Roman Democracy and European cities. But the East Wing was nothing like the other buildings. I was awestruck. I walked slowly up the rise of stairs to the mezzanine level, taking in the sharp angles and brightness. I'd left my schoolmates behind in the other building, to their games of running past classics, fooling around on the grand staircases, and eluding our teachers. I'd wandered into a new space. A place that calmed me in its clean modernism. It was unlike anything I'd ever seen back in Texas, and nothing like my new home in Georgetown.

Calming me.

A sanctuary.

I took a seat on one of the benches on the mezzanine and watched the mobile floating overhead. I didn't know the names of any of the artists that day, although I would learn them over the summer, taking refuge from the heat in the cool sanctuaries of art. I would learn that the mobile overhead was a Calder, commissioned for the building. A permanent installation. I would learn of the Matisse cutouts with their limited viewing schedule to preserve their colors. I would smile at the Modigliani portraiture and the Rothko blocks of paint and the white plaster dancing girls I would know as the Segal.

I didn't know any of those things that day. I was mesmerized by the space, the silence, and the beauty of it all. A new world.

"You like the Calder, Caleb?" Mrs. Spaulding asked as she sat on the bench next to me.

"Excuse me, ma'am?"

"The mobile. It's by an artist named Alexander Calder."

"Oh. It seems so big and heavy, but it appears to float there. It'd be a disaster if it fell," I said as I gazed at the floating panels of brightly colored metal.

Mrs. Spaulding laughed gently at my comment.

"I don't think it will fall, Caleb. It was commissioned for this building. I believe it is a part of the structure."

We both sat on the bench watching the mobile float overhead. It made sense to me that the mobile was commissioned for the building, as it seemed to fit the atrium perfectly.

"Caleb, Principal Montgomery has taken the other children across the way to the Hirshhorn and we should join them. It's our last stop for the day."

"Are there going to be more Calders at the Hirshhorn, ma'am?"

"There might be. . . . I'm certain of at least one in the sculpture garden." With this we stood and walked down the sweep of stairs to the doors at street level.

Across the green of the Mall was a building just as beautiful as the East Wing. A circle of pink cast granite with no exterior windows, suspended on sculptural pillars with a fountain in the center.

The Hirshhorn Museum and Sculpture Garden.

Principal Montgomery and the other children were standing by the fountain awaiting our arrival. The other kids were restless and joking around as Mrs. Spaulding and I walked toward them. Once James spotted us he expressed his regret at my arrival.

"Damn it, I thought that maybe you'd been kidnapped. Then again, who would want ya?" The other kids laughed and James stood with a self-congratulatory smile on his face. Principal Montgomery snapped her fingers and pointed at James, a warning that he shouldn't be so proud of himself.

"Try to stick with the group the rest of the day, Caleb," Principal Montgomery said as Mrs. Spaulding placed a comforting hand on my shoulder. "Everyone, we meet back here by the fountain at two forty-five, then we will walk back to the school and you will be dismissed from there. Please respect the building and the art as you are representing our school and your family. Do not give me reason to punish you on your last week before the summer." With those words Principal Montgomery led us toward the revolving doors to enter the building. Standing just outside, she counted the other students off in threes and fours to enter. Mrs. Spaulding and I were the last to go through the door and enter the round granite building. I soon found that it held the same majesty as the East Wing. Clean, cool, modern, and silent.

The other children went up the escalators to the galleries, but walking away from Mrs. Spaulding, I started in the cool basement, at a small gallery of the museum's temporary pieces outside the doors to the auditorium. The paintings captivated me. Bright colors, multiple textures, expressions from abstract to primitive. All of them so full of emotion. Alive.

Then I rode the escalator to the second-floor galleries. The inner circle of the round housed the Hirshhorn's collection of sculptures, including wireworks by Calder and Picasso, the mixed media boxes of Louise Nevelson, and ceiling-mounted installations by Miró. I walked through the collection, carefully examining every piece. The Hirshhorn was another sanctuary. The pieces kept there were artifacts, the unearthed remains of people who saw the world differently. Flashes of color started to catch my eye from the galleries that made the outer wall of the circular sanctuary. I drifted toward those rooms without windows.

Modern paintings broadly spaced on the walls.

Splatters of Pollock, blocks of Rothko, the complicated simplicity of Jasper Johns, but one painting caught me and drew me in. I was entranced.

Two square panels of canvas hung with the sides touching. Almost seven feet high and fourteen feet wide. It covered the wall. One a field of stark white, the other a field of the brightest pink. A single image repeated in rows, seven across and twelve down on each canvas. Lips in a seductive smile. Black on the white field. Black, white, and red on the pink field. One hundred sixty-eight sets of lips anticipating a kiss.

I walked to the wall and read the card.

Marilyn Monroe's Lips by Andy Warhol. Synthetic polymer, silk-screen ink, and pencil on canvas.

I remained a foot away from the painting, studying a single set of lips rendered in photographic perfection. The fine graining of ink pushed through a screen. The slightest imperfections to each set of lips in the repetition. The ink was heavier in some, barely transferred to the canvas in the others. I counted the lips up close to double-check my first count. One hundred sixty-eight sets of lips on the wall. Beautiful repetition of the same image. But the imperfections made each set of lips a bit different.

I sat on the sleek leather bench in the center of the room, gazing at the painting from a distance. From there the imperfections faded and it was perfect repetition. Beautiful monotony. I sat and studied the painting. The room silent around me. The other paintings faded from my line of sight and the lips hovered on the wall in front of me.

Simple.

Beautiful.

True.

"Do you know whose lips those are?"

The security guard's question rattled me out of my trance.

"No sir, I don't."

"Those are the lips of Marilyn Monroe. They called her a screen goddess; I guess they still do." The guard sat on the bench next to me.

"She's in movies?"

"Just a few. Before she overdosed."

"Overdosed?"

"They say she took too many pills, but I suppose I shouldn't be telling you that." The guard stood up and straightened his jacket. "You here on a school trip?"

"Yes, sir." As I answered the guard I heard my name called from the passageway to the gallery.

"Looks like it's time to get back to school, Caleb," the guard said as he touched the brim of his cap.

I rose from the bench and faced Mrs. Spaulding.

"Yes, ma'am."

"Principal Montgomery is gathering the other children in the lobby for the walk back to school and we should join them."

"Yes, ma'am. But have you seen any more paintings like this one?" I pointed toward the lips on the wall.

"Ah, a Warhol. Yes, I've seen a few. Do you like this one?"

"Oh yes. There's something beautiful about it."

On the last day of school, Mrs. Spaulding had asked my father to come in for a meeting. I waited on a bench in the hall while they talked. My father enjoyed meetings with anyone. It gave him the opportunity to chat people up and prove his influence. He could do some name-dropping and boost his own ego. Meetings helped my father assert his greatness.

However, school meetings limited his ability to do all of this, as the expectation of them was that they would be about my education. Usually, the job of attending school meetings was passed off on my stepmother. But Mrs. Spaulding had asked specifically for my father on the last day. The meeting lasted about forty-five minutes. Certainly the first twenty were spent on my father's favorite subject: his importance.

The door opened and my father appeared holding a few books, which he handed to me.

"We're supposed to try letting you be an artist." He motioned for me to follow him.

The Art of Andy Warhol.

The Corcoran School of Art Summer Youth Programs.

The summer art program was the beginning of what became years of transformation and discovery for me. The Corcoran allowed younger students to explore the arts in a studio setting over the summer break from traditional schools. I picked classes in drawing, screen printing, and mixed-media collage.

On the days I didn't have classes or permission to use the studios I spent my time in my sanctuaries, the museums and galleries. Learning about and being around art became my obsession. There I felt comfortable and safe.

The paintings and the art supplies became my friends.

Drawing was my least favorite of the classes. It was tedious work but a required foundation for the rest. The instructors stressed the importance of having a basic conceptual sketch before moving forward with a project, but I knew that I wanted to work as a Pop artist. I wanted the immediacy of the images around me. I couldn't sketch in photo-realism. The images I wanted to create didn't have shadow, depth, or contouring. Drafting was the necessary penance I had to endure before I was allowed to use the screens and presses.

Mixed media was more fun than drawing. I could take things from magazines, snapshots, and random items I collected and build them up on canvas or board. Mixing textures and visual ideas. Combining elements into otherwise impossible scenarios. The medium felt the most like my own thoughts. Playing Dr. Frankenstein with found objects. Jumbled and chaotic. Less discipline and more a free-form fusion of painting and sculpture. Collages built out of my thoughts.

But my primary reason for being at the Corcoran was my truest love, screen printing. The medium Andy had taken from the world of commercial art and made Pop. The process by which you could create multiple and limitless works of art. Photo emulsion and stencils applied on a screen to squeegee art into beautiful repetition. The creation of monotonous and perfect images to cluster on the walls or split apart so that everyone could have a piece of beauty to consider his own.

I'd started to read Warhol's *The Philosophy of Andy Warhol* and was inspired by the idea that art should be open and accessible from its production through to distribution. Everyone should be able to have something beautiful in their personal space. A most democratic approach to art. Working in the style and methods of Warhol's Factory calmed me, especially being able to make multiple copies of the images.

I wished I could make multiples of other things.

I wanted to be able to make friends.

Discovering creative vehicles was important; but art school brought me something even more important: contemporaries. Other students more like me and less like the kids at the day school.

Through them I learned that expression, true artistic expression, was something you could apply to yourself as well as to your art. The creation of your own identity was as much an art form as a painting, a collage, or a silk screen. I studied my schoolmates at the Corcoran as much as any of the other techniques I was taught.

The upperclassmen moving their works into the galleries by freight elevator in the mornings, the assorted painters and sculptors with their punk rock sensibilities, the other printmakers hovering above screens in their thrift-store jackets and haystacked hairstyles; they gathered in the halls during breaks to smoke, drink coffee, and talk about their visions.

None of them would have fit in at the day school.

I watched them and learned from them.

It was Trea, another printmaker, who told me about peroxide. She wore her hair in a shocking white bob with russet-brown roots. Curiously, I asked how she had turned it that color. Simple peroxide from the drugstore run through her hair in the shower, she said. She assured me that on my dish-water blond it would work quickly. I picked up a bottle of peroxide at the drugstore and started the rinsing trick the day she told me about it. Over the first few weeks the rinses turned my hair a full spectrum of gold to yellow and finally to a pale yellow. At the pale yellow point Trea shared another secret—blue rinse. From the supermarket aisle with laundry soap came a small blue bottle of Bluette, a pigment added to rinse water to remove yellow from towels and bedsheets. When added to shampoo the blue pigment neutralized the last bits of yellow from my peroxide-faded hair.

The silvered Warhol mop.

My art school friends thought the effect was fabulous.

It was good to be fabulous in an environment that accepted and encouraged you to be different.

Unique.

Accepted.

love (friendship)

After my summer at the Corcoran, I started my second and last year at the day school. I did no better fitting in with the other kids as an eighth grader than I had the previous year as the new kid in the seventh grade. I had changed quickly in the art school environment and not the way that would go unde-tected at the day school. I'd transformed myself into a grade school- clone of my hero. A pint-size Warhol. My summer with the art school crowd had given me the confidence to not only be different, but also to express myself in an extreme fashion.

So shocking was the art I had made of myself that James and the other children dismissed me with just one word on our first day back at school.

Freak.

The new label was as much attention as James paid me in the new school year. It stuck, but James had a new object for his scorn and ridicule. This school year had presented James with a target in the form of a new student.

Aaron.

He wasn't average like the other children. Aaron possessed the looks and charisma that would have him labeled a pretty boy. Beauty that implied tenderness. There was a darkness to all his features. Hair and eyes of the deepest browns were matched to olive skin that appeared permanently tanned. The beauty contrasted with a rugged physical quality that I imagined made him good at any sport. His bushy eyebrows peeked out from behind a wavy mane of hair that was as thick as the eyelashes that gave the appearance of black eyeliner. In spite of his striking looks, he was very shy, in the same way that I was. Soft-spoken. Withdrawn. All of these things brought on insult and ridicule from James.

In appearance Aaron was the opposite of me.

He was the most beautiful boy I'd ever seen.

And he became the first friend I ever had.

Our shyness made it a slow-growing friendship from the start. Neither of us cared to spend recess with the rest of the kids, choosing instead to take refuge in the library with our books. Actually speaking to each other took us a few weeks. We started on opposite sides of the room, each moving a bit closer every few days. I usually studied the art books or worked on my French homework and Aaron passed the hour with his sketchbook. Stealing glances at each other and looking away if we happened to look at the same time. The pattern became routine and would have lasted the entire year as a silent friendship had not Aaron chosen one day to sit at the same table, right across from me.

My heartbeat felt quick and I didn't know how to speak. I thought I should've moved to another table. I couldn't have moved anyway. I was frozen in place and if I moved I surely would have bungled something and then Aaron would have become like the others, knowing what a freak I was.

"What are you reading?"

His voice matched everything about him. Soft but dark. It had already started to change, taking on a deep quality and not the odd cracking of my own voice. Since I was still a year younger than everyone else my voice hadn't fully changed.

"Reading?" My voice cracked on the single word. Nervous about beginning the conversation. I feared that I'd ruin the beauty of his company with any response. I was terrified that he would see my awkwardness and dismiss me. If I ruined the moment he, too, would have known me as the freak. He would be just like the other kids.

His eyebrows knit themselves into an odd expression. It was like a smile offered to me as he pointed at my French textbook.

"Oh, yeah. Studying. For French class." My words were choppy. The simplest response was hard to string together in front of him.

"Hmm. That's cool."

He opened his sketchbook and left me to study my French. I looked into the spine of my book and moved my eyes across the page. I couldn't see the words. My eyes moved just to give the impression that I was studying while I considered every detail of the conversation we'd had. I hadn't bungled it. I answered the question and he thought my answer was cool. I wasn't a freak.

It was a start.

I learned about Aaron gradually through our short exchanges during recess. Sitting across from each other at the same table. Aaron sketching and me with my books.

I learned that he was from New Jersey.

His parents had recently divorced.

His father worked for a congressman.

He and his father shared an apartment in the lower part of Georgetown. Aaron spoke of his father more like a roommate than a parent. He even called his father by his first name, Chuck. Chuck left him alone most of the time, spending evenings out drinking with other congressional staffers or out on dates. Aaron missed New Jersey but his mother didn't feel like she could raise a teenage boy on her own. She had sent him to live with Chuck and attend the day school, and he spent only the summers back up north.

He played soccer on Saturday mornings with a youth league team that had matches on the southwest waterfront. Aaron loved soccer. Mondays were spent telling me of his matches and awesome plays on the field. Soccer stories brought out his most animated side and were the stories with the most smiles. His tales of being the champion on the field made us both smile.

The only love that compared to soccer for Aaron was comic books. He collected comics about heroes. Superman. Spider-Man. Batman. His favorite were the X-men, a collective of mutants with various superpowers. Aaron filled his sketchbooks with his own ideas for comics, showing me his drawings now and then, trying to explain the superheroes he had imagined. I didn't always understand the appeal of the comic story lines, but I liked the idea that Aaron was an artist and comic books did have the same vivid graphic style of Pop Art. The art was something Aaron and I had in common.

Whereas our ideas about music couldn't have been more different. I loved the New Wave imports and stayed up late to watch them on the cable music video shows. I sat in the den mesmerized by *Friday Night Videos* and *Night Flight*. The flickering television screen broadcasted the great synth-pop acts in five-minute films. I loved the images. I loved the clothes and hairstyles of Britpop. I wanted to copy the New Romantics style of Duran Duran. I wanted to be beautiful like Nick Rhodes.

Aaron dismissed my musical tastes as crap. His music was rougher. He liked the bands with lots of hair and spandex. On the subject of music we never found common ground. We exchanged tapes, trying to get the other to share something there. I tried to like Dokken, Ratt, and the other bands Aaron liked, but it was all just noise to me.

Through our days in the empty school library we talked about all of these things. Even with a few differences we kept talking. Only in the library, with no one else around, but we were talking. The library was so infrequently used it didn't even merit an attendant. I made my first real friend in that library.

"What soap do you use?"

"Soap?"

"In the shower."

Aaron arrived every morning still damp from the shower. His wavy hair heavy around his head, clean and smelling of soap. Through the day the waves would get fuller on his head and the clean smell lingered and became a part of him. It became familiar and comforted me when he was near. I wanted to know how that comfort was made.

My father had terrible skin as a teenager. Genetics were expected to provide me with the same problem. My father's face was marked by scars from his problem skin, so my stepmother was vigilant about my not having troubled teenage skin. I was taken to the dermatologist and estheticians to prevent it. Every morning and night I had to wash my face with special soap. Burning, stinging soap that smelled of tar and other chemicals. Again, it was a matter of appearances. The smell that lingered with me was sterile, chemical. A different kind of clean, not the perfumed clean with which Aaron greeted me in the library.

"Striped. Green striped soap, I don't know the name. Why?"

"It smells nice." I went back to my French words and Aaron watched me for a moment, then returned to his sketching.

I stopped at the drugstore on the way home and opened boxes until I found a green striped bar of soap. *Irish Spring*. I put the bar of soap into my book bag and walked home. I showered with the striped soap every night so that I could sleep with that smell instead of the chemical smell I knew as my own.

The scent made me feel secure, as though Aaron were near. I wondered about actual proximity. Could he make me sane?

Or was it just green soap that made me feel that I might belong somewhere?

Irish Spring let me sleep well.

But my skin started showing signs of trouble, so my stepmother took me to more dermatologists. I started dry ice treatments that burned away the traces of the green striped soap. The treatments continued and made my skin brittle and pale. I couldn't sleep at night without the scent of the soap I kept hidden under the sink in my bathroom. The secret showers made trips to the dermatologist a constant of my youth; my stepmother blamed the genetics I shared with my mother and father, but it was the soap I couldn't live without.

therapy (transformation)

As my appearance changed and emulation caused me to look more like Warhol, I felt more at ease. I was an outcast and an object of scorn, but at least of my own design. I was no longer harassed about my accent or the way I dressed, but I was sneered at and dismissed as a freak. I had run enough peroxide through my hair to turn it from dishwater blond to platinum. I had avoided the sun, so I was pasty white, and I had swabbed my face with acetone until it had a brittle and chalky appearance. I did my best to smooth out my accent when I could, trying to drop the Southern drawl and replace it with a flat monotone like Andy's. Once again, I was making mistakes in the seen-and-heard department. Not the mistakes I had started with, but a new set of them. The kind of mistakes that get a person called a freak by people who can't see self-expression as an art.

Not only did *freak* catch on as my new nickname, it ran rampant through the school. With the exception of Aaron, the other children wrote me off. My father was called to the school for another meeting. This time Principal Montgomery had decided that I was just too different from the other children and she was going to have to intervene. The first step in helping me was meeting with my father. As expected, my father came for the meeting, chatted up the faculty about his accomplishments, and left with some recommendations for my education and care.

Apparently, in 1984, the treatment for being a social outcast was therapy.

I was referred to Dr. Elliot Moore.

Dr. Moore had an office on the ground floor of his R Street brownstone, just three blocks from the Dupont Circle Metro. My first meeting with Dr. Moore was with my father on a Saturday morning.

The doctor sat behind his large cherry desk with my father and me in armchairs facing him. I didn't speak much during our first meeting; my father did all the talking. I looked around the room at the collection of books and memorabilia. It seemed to me that the doctor had traveled a great deal. Scattered around the office were carved wooden figures that looked African, tapestries in the patterns and colors of Morocco, an ashtray that said DRUGSTORE PUBLICIS, and framed photos of the doctor with various skylines as the backdrop. The photos could easily have been of an aged Ernest Hemingway; the doctor shared an uncanny resemblance to him. All he needed was the fishing cap. I searched the walls and shelves for a fishing cap or elephant rifle. Some kind of proof that we were in the lost study of Papa Hemingway so that I could argue with my father that I didn't need to return there for therapy. But no fishing cap, no rifle. Just a graying furry man, my father, and me, the freak.

From that first meeting, my father relinquished his parenting responsibilities to the doctor. They had agreed before we left the office that all of my problems, punishments, and reprimands would be handled by Dr. Moore. As Freud had the power to manipulate and distort Dora, Dr. Elliot Moore would be free to tinker with my adolescent mind courtesy of my father's indifference to the task of parenting.

My second meeting at the brownstone with the doctor involved a battery of tests. Word associations, inkblots, blocks, puzzles, multiple choice questions, images, and drawing the meaning of certain words in pictures. It was an entire afternoon of testing. The results of the test determined what course his therapy would take for me. The testing was a technical necessity in order to start treatment. It was to reveal how my mind had been arranging its thoughts and thereby making me different.

In what my father would later find an unorthodox move, the doctor shared the findings of the tests with me privately first, without my father present.

I was different from most boys and always would be. A battery of tests had proven it. Nothing would make the difference go away, since the doctor didn't believe there was anything to fix. He felt that my happiness would come through encouragement, acceptance, and education. There would be no reprimands for behavior, only discussions and education. Therapy moved from the ground floor of the brownstone and into the world.

Therapy didn't resemble therapy after the testing; it had become more like dating. Dr. Moore and I would spend weekends having coffee and hitting the galleries and museums. From time to time we might take in a good art house movie or one of the series of films showing at the East Wing of the National Gallery.

The Warhol short films were my favorites. Reels of film made with the Warhol Superstars living the life to which I wanted to escape. Artistic genius and beauty in collaboration on film. Edie, Gerard, and boys dressed as girls as living Pop Art on the screen, and not a single one of them was being chaperoned through this art by a Hemingway look-alike. The doctor would show me more of the life I wanted, but I had to endure his company to see it.

I met the owners of the independent bookshops and vintage stores around Dupont Circle and Adams Morgan. The doctor was well known in his neighborhood and, after being introduced, I had become known around the neighborhood, too. If an interesting art book appeared in one of the shops, it would be put aside until I had the chance to look it over; a vintage motorcycle jacket in my size was held until I'd had a chance to try it on. All of the people the doctor introduced me to appreciated just how unique I was. It seemed that under his care I had a privileged life. Life not unlike the textbook family life, just with a different cast of characters.

One of the first reprimands entrusted to the doctor was when I was caught smoking. My father had seen me walking down the street from our house with a cigarette in my hand one afternoon. I had been smoking cigarettes taken from his desk since my time at the Corcoran and had just started buying packs of my own at the corner store. My father smoked Marlboro Reds, but I'd come to prefer the mentholated taste of Newports. Menthol cigarettes seemed to jumpstart the process of becoming a lifetime smoker. Creating an intense tingling sensation on my sinuses and lungs, the taste and strength of the Newports hooked me within hours. My nose burned with the cool menthol so I chain-smoked them to keep that thrill going. The only downside was that I reeked of smoke all of the time.

Dr. Moore asked me about the smoking. I said it made me feel less fidgety and it gave me something to do. I enjoyed the taste of the cool menthol smoke. I gave him the simplest of reasons for my new habit. He considered these things and warned me of the health risks and the counterculture implications of cigarettes. He warned me of their addictive nature. He said that my father had entrusted him with the responsibility of fully informing me of the dangerous choice I was making. Then we decided together that smoking was an acceptable vice for an aspiring artist like myself. Therapy didn't mean I wouldn't make dangerous choices. I would make choices of my own, provided with the necessary information.

I arrived at the brownstone one afternoon to find Aaron sitting on the sofa in the office. He, too, had been referred to the doctor due to his problems making friends at the day school. The doctor explained that he thought Aaron and I would benefit from sharing our sessions. If we learned to interact more with each other, then we might have an easier time with the other students. I nodded, even though having Aaron there on the sofa made me nervous.

Aaron was quiet and nervous as well. Sitting next to him on the sofa was his sketchbook. He guarded it with one hand until Dr. Moore brought it up in conversation.

"Aaron is an artist, too, Caleb. Did you know that?"

"Yes, sir. He draws comics."

I had never asked to see Aaron's work. He had shown them to me during some of our times in the library, but I'd never examined their contents. I knew that Aaron spent most of his free time drawing in the sketchbooks and I didn't want to intrude upon his private pleasure in it. Yes, I was curious. I just didn't want to see anything until he wanted to show me.

"Would you like to see his drawings? He's rather good. I think you might like them, Caleb."

I looked at Aaron on the sofa, his hand still guarding the sketchbook. I looked at the doctor, with his eyes resting on me, awaiting an answer.

"Yes, sir. I think I would."

Aaron stood from the sofa and carried his most prized sketchbook to the desk. We stood with it sitting on the desk, surrounded by the three of us. I opened the book to the first page, Aaron nervously glanced away, and the doctor stood silently looking over my shoulder. I carefully turned the pages, taking in the images, seeing a story emerge.

The pages of the book were filled with a grid work of felt marker lines. No words, just images and storyboards. Aaron's life in comic book style, like Pop Art. Within a few pages I picked up the story from the images in the black-and-white grids. A move to a new city, a new school. Dark, shaded images. Loneliness. The other kids at school joined in unfriendly clusters. Aaron with his head hung low. Soccer matches outside of school. The champion on the field. The library. Me. Our time in the library rendered in the frames. My walks home alone. My father's town house.

Had he followed me? I glanced up from the book, but Aaron looked away nervously. I continued to flip through the pages.

Our friendship in superhero rendering with great detail given to every afternoon in the library. Time-consuming documentation. The figures no longer dark and shaded. Smiles instead of heads hung low.

I closed the book and looked at Aaron. He looked around the room to avoid me.

"His drawings are quite good, aren't they, Caleb?"

"Yes, they're amazing. I didn't know."

With the compliment, Aaron finally looked at me. We locked into a gaze; his brows crinkled into a sheepish smile.

"Thanks."

Then I had a best friend who would join my therapy sessions. Learn everything about me. Share secrets.

Aaron heard all about my summer of strolling the galleries and museums, my sanctuaries. I told him all about my last summer of art classes at the Corcoran. The doctor and I caught him up on the books I'd been reading and recommended some of them to him. The doctor made a point of telling me that Aaron had been tested as well.

Aaron was different, too, different like me.

Aaron enjoyed art. He was a bit intrigued by my fascination with Warhol, though to him Lichtenstein was the Pop artist of note.

His sketchbooks were better than any Lichtenstein, though. Aaron told the full story without any words.

As with most of my adolescent discoveries, my first kiss was in therapy. Because it was therapy we were aware of doctor-patient confidentiality. We stood advised that we didn't ever have to tell our parents what happened in therapy and we should never tell anyone else outside of the brownstone what activities we engaged in there. We often talked about the world's great secret societies throughout history and how important they were. Many of the world's great artists, leaders, and thinkers were members of such societies, and one day both of us might achieve such greatness. Then we could attribute our successes to the secrets we were able to keep.

Gertrude Stein had founded such a society in Paris. Lord Byron led a similar secret society in England. Warhol's Factory was an experiment in society even though the fame of it had made it an impossible secret to keep. Socrates had practiced as the leader of one, and we could never forget Allen Ginsberg and his society of beats.

We would indeed howl in that brownstone. Our years of secret experiments started with a kiss.

Liberties are taken in calling it my first real kiss, as everything about it was pretty well staged and coached. It's not the kind of thing they teach you in prep school, so it's a job they have to outsource. I'd later be told I was gifted in the making-out department, though developmentally I might have gotten stuck there. The early kissing coaching must have been good.

Dr. Moore supervised my first kiss. Aaron shared it.

We were both still reserved in school. The doctor felt that if we could become more comfortable with each other we might find a way to become more assertive with our schoolmates. The doctor's theory was that if Aaron and I developed an intimacy free of judgment, it would give us both the strength to deal with not fitting in at school. We'd form solidarity against the kids there. At least, that was the plan presented to us.

We were both very nervous that day. We'd shared time in therapy before, getting to know each other more than we had already in the library.

My nostrils filled with the faint smell of the green striped soap as our lips touched. Soft warmth pressed to my lips. I pulled away slowly and Aaron followed me to continue the kiss a moment longer. We parted and my eyes opened to see his brown eyes looking back at me. Everything outside that moment vanished. It all melted away in a blur. His eyes had not a trace of fear in them . . . none of the nervousness he usually carried. His eyes looked at me with only certainty. I could hear a muffled murmur of sound, the doctor's voice, unintelligible through the pounding in my ears. The pounding coming from inside me. *Thump, thump, thump.* I blinked my eyes to break Aaron's gaze and tried to hear again.

"You boys are pretty good at that." The doctor chuckled.

"Yes. He is."

I stood silent, shocked by Aaron's reply.

Had we been like other boys we would have experimented with games of spin the bottle at the houses of our classmates. But birthday parties and sleepovers were the types of things we only heard about at school as we were never invited to them. The doctor's brownstone served as the only place where we could experience such things. We knew we were hidden from view there, and outside of therapy we avoided acknowledging things like the kiss.

My first Polaroid camera was a gift from Dr. Moore. A used SX-70 he'd found in a thrift store. A folding camera loaded with the Polaroid instant film. It had basic focus and contrast control. The images captured by its lens emerged in just moments. Close shots remained fuzzy and primitive with the skin tones and texture smoothed out, but deep contrast remained on the film. The same type of refinements and improvements of reality that I had seen in Warhol's silk-screen works. I carried the SX-70 folded in my book bag, always with me. I spent my allowance on cartridges of instant film for documenting my world. Anything that looked like it could be Pop Art was captured by the shutter. I made images to carry with me or file away in a shoe box on my bookshelf. A photo diary of my world, through my eyes. With that junk-store camera, Dr. Moore had opened my eyes.

Seeing through the lens started to become a part of my day-to-day life and I focused on the everyday. I clicked the shutter on the shelves at grocery and drugstores, inspired by the Campbell's soup cans and the Coca-Cola bottles that had launched Pop. I noticed hubcaps and architectural elements around me as I framed them tightly in the viewer to create abstract compositions. I looked for beauty in the things that often go unnoticed. That lens allowed me to see the beauty from behind the safe remove of a steel-and-leather-covered folding camera.

I fell in love with groceries, bars of soap, hubcaps, awnings, parking meters, and doorways. The images saved in a shoe box. Admiring glimpses of everyday objects captured on the instant film. I found my fascinations frozen on the film and loved them. I learned to see with affection.

I became a voyeur.

love (intimacy)

People change when seen through a lens.

My camera went everywhere with me. Discovering things, people, characters. I made a large collection of snapshots, just random things. Dr. Moore had suggested that I find a model, a human subject. He said I should photograph the people I knew in the same way I looked at groceries and hubcaps. And Dr. Moore thought Aaron would be the best first subject.

Up until I took the first photographs, I'd considered Aaron my best friend. He was the person that was closest to me. Through the lens I discovered him as separate from me. I actually saw him as a rare beauty. I could see the tenderness of his expression, hiding some pain beneath his innocence and how his life had corrupted him. He was tough on the outside but his eyes carried a kind of hurt.

We started with simple candid images, as random as when I would stumble across a street sign or manhole cover I felt the need to document. At first Aaron was uncomfortable with the occasional clicking, but he began to relax and became both more comfortable and more expressive.

Every contour of his being appeared on the instant film. Pieces emerged as the film developed, to be carried in my pocket, filed away in boxes and photo albums. He was always a willing subject for my snapshots.

And through the lens the love was returned. Those hurting eyes trusting, gazing directly at me as though there were no camera.

By staying on my side of the lens, I was allowed closeness without having to touch. After our time with the doctor neither of us wanted to. Not in that way. Something about touching now felt taboo, uncomfortable. It excited and terrified me. I knew that other people didn't feel that way about their best friends. I knew the feelings were another thing that made me not normal. I didn't want to be so different. The only times I felt that I wasn't were with Dr. Moore and whenever Aaron and I were alone.

The snapshots were a collaboration between us. We were experimenting and making art together, though separated by the lens. As we grew closer the photographs became more intimate. I kept a shoe box on my bookshelf filled with pictures of Aaron changing, growing stronger, puberty forcing him toward manhood.

He became my muse. He captivated me.

All the beauty of the world was held in his smoldering brown eyes, turbulent waves of hair, smooth golden skin, and the sculptural lines of his athletic body. His perfection was uninhibited and unknown to him.

Beauty.

Raw beauty.

The art we created was the progressing mixed-media collaboration of his form, my film, and our trust. His body constantly improved, my vision and skill with the camera was refined. There was partnership and love affair in the images we created.

On the advice of the doctor, my father bought me a 35mm camera. It was an Olympus OM-10, the most basic manual model in that camera format. Whereas the Polaroids captured the vaguest idea of an image, the Olympus captured every last detail. No longer making just snapshots, a better camera shifted our projects to the realm of fine art. A new inspiration occurred to me and Aaron consented.

The fine art nude.

I prepared by making a meticulous study of every black-and-white image I found in bookstores and galleries. Whether they were books of nudes or street scenes, I wanted to understand the light and how it was used in the photograph.

Mapplethorpe. Brassaï. Weston. Avedon. Doisneau.

I studied the contrast and the illumination. I visited camera shops and asked questions about black-and-white film and its chemistry. I took the Metro back down to the Corcoran and asked the instructors as many questions as they would answer for me between classes.

I learned that the images would have to be shot on a slow film with high key lighting if I wanted the shadows and highlights of Brassaï's Paris prints. This was accomplished with a simple floodlight in a silver reflector that I bought from the hardware store on M Street. A black sheet tacked to the basement wall was a backdrop. I lit the room with only the floodlight, positioned high and to the right of the background. I set the camera on a tripod and framed the black sheet through the lens. I locked all the doors as Aaron sat on the edge of my twin bed.

"Are you ready to start?"

"Yeah, I guess so," he nervously replied. He stood and pulled his T-shirt over his head, folding it roughly and placing it on the bed. He unbuckled his jeans and slid his briefs and then tube socks to the floor. All of this, too, was folded roughly and placed on top of the T-shirt. He crossed the room and took his spot in front of the black backdrop, his body tense with his hands clasped in front of him, hiding himself. The last bit of shyness left to be overcome.

"I'm going to take a Polaroid to check the light, okay?"

"Okay."

"Are you warm enough? I can turn on a heater."

"I'm fine. Let's just take the pictures." His eyes glanced up from his bowed head with the whisper.

I framed his head, shoulders, and torso in the Polaroid viewfinder, allowing him his shyness for the test shot. I pulled the tab of film from the camera and checked my watch. While waiting for the instant film to develop I brought him a blanket. He wrapped it loosely around his waist and waited as I peeled the film apart.

The high key lighting added more definition to his physique in the photo. Half of his form was sculpted with the light while the other half receded into the background with shadow. The darkness obscured his face from the light, which was unable to break through his mane of curls. Only the line of his jaw and the plane of his cheekbone caught the illumination. The cap of his shoulder, the upper curve of his chest, and a crescent of nipple emerged from the shadows. I glanced up from the image and smiled at him as he stood there patiently in the blanket.

"It's okay?" His eyebrows scrunched into a worried query.

"You're a statue, Aaron." I crossed to show him the film.

He tilted his head to the side as he studied the picture. It was as though he didn't recognize himself. He studied the light as I did. He studied his own body, tucking the blanket more firmly so that he could explore the curves of his form with his free hand, comparing what he felt to the image he saw on the film.

"Are you happy with the light?"

"Yeah. Are you ready to shoot the rest?"

He nodded his head and handed me back the Polaroid. I took my position on the other side of the tripod and framed my first shot in the viewfinder. His full form, from head to toe, in the shadows and light. He tugged at the blanket and let the cotton pool around his feet while still clasping his hands to hide his cock. I turned the lens to refine the focus. I waited and watched him through the lens. Aaron inhaled a deep breath and slowly exhaled so that his body relaxed with the air leaving his chest. Without any direction from me he unclasped his hands and let his arms fall to his sides. I pressed the button and listened to the click of the shutter.

I advanced the film to the next frame with a pull of my thumb. With the next twenty-three frames I traveled along his body as though it were a landscape. Three full body shots: profile, front, and rear. Then I mapped his form in parts.

He was almost a year older than me, so his body was more mature than my own. I made a study of the masculinity on the film. The curve of his chest with the first sprouts of hair around his nipples. The square of shoulder with the dark coarse hair at his armpit. His jaw with the beginnings of stubble; he had started to shave every other day. A dense cover of pubic hair abundant at the base of a line from his belly button and a cover of dark hair down his strong soccer-playing legs. He had powerful legs. They were the legs of a field champion. His victories there had made his body firm, with every part of him finely tuned and full of purpose. Made for strength and only incidentally for beauty. With every click of the shutter I studied the parts. Through my lens there were twenty-one pieces to his beauty. His shyness faded as the time passed and he patiently modeled for two hours. Intuiting my gaze, he knew how to breathe to best show the parts on which I lingered. He shifted his weight to tighten the roundness of his hip and buttocks, breathed slowly and deeply to broaden his chest and define his abs. His raised his head proudly, not letting it bow to the floor. He watched me as intensely as I watched him, sometimes with a smile, sometimes with a smirk.

I carefully turned the crank on the bottom of the camera to rewind the film after the last frame had been shot. Aaron pulled on his jeans, tugged the T-shirt over his head, and sat on the bed. Disheveled, he looked at me and crinkled his brow.

"Do you think they'll look anything like the test shot?"

"I hope they do. The test shot was awesome." I pulled the film from the camera and set it on my desk. I glanced at the test shot again, studying the light. I handed the Polaroid to Aaron.

"You should keep this one."

He looked at the image and looked back at me. He bit into his bottom lip and the crinkled brow gave way to a very happy smile.

I intended to send the film from our nude shoot away in a mailer, so I had left the canister on my desk until I had time to go to the camera store and buy one. I always seemed to re-member right before bed, just as I would glance over and see the canister on my desk. I never got around to it during the day, though.

But the film finally did get developed. My father found the canister on my desk and took it to the drugstore to be processed. I was surprised to find him waiting for me when I came home from school one afternoon.

My father sat at the dining room table. In front of him were a glass of scotch, his pack of cigarettes, a full ashtray, and a stack of black-and-white prints. My photos. Aaron's nudes.

"Can you explain what this is about?" He set the stack of photos at the center of the dining room table.

"Just some pictures I took."

He glared at me before his fury unleashed itself.

"No, Caleb! Not just some pictures. What's wrong with you? Do you have any idea how much explaining I had to do? I had to tell the man at the drugstore that my son is some kind of weirdo. These are not just pictures, Caleb. They thought I was the pervert! But, no. I had to convince them that my son is the queer!" His voice and anger grew louder, his face turned red, and his hands trembled. "Not just pictures, Caleb. Don't do it ever again! Are you just trying to end up a flaming faggot?"

"NO! They're just fucking pictures! Like art!" I yelled back at him.

I never shouted or cursed at my father. When I did both those things, he grabbed the photos from the table, stuffed them back into the envelope, and stormed out of the room. I thought he was going to burn them without letting me see them. From what I had glimpsed at the top of the stack, they were beautiful photographs and possibly fine art. I was certain I would never see them again, which hurt more than the word *faggot*. I tried to remember the sequence in which we had taken the pictures. I tried to imagine what would come next in the stack.

I didn't have to imagine for long. Two days later I walked into Dr. Moore's study to see the doctor and Aaron standing at his desk, on which all twenty-four prints were laid out in a grid. As with every other problem of mine, my father had turned this one over to the doctor for reprimand duty. I crossed the room and circled the desk to see the photos. Aaron and the doctor parted in silence as I moved to the center to study the tableau.

In front of me lay breathtaking beauty. Each frame was a different view of desire I didn't fully understand yet. The expanse of a shoulder dropping into tight biceps. A line traced from his ear, down his neck to the valley that connected to his shoulder. Another photo was a close-up shot of his stomach with the whirls of dark hair that softened into a shadowy line that disappeared into blackness at the middle of the print. The bone of his pelvis caught bright highlights next to a darker dense forest of pubic hair, his thick penis fading into the shadows that the light couldn't reach. His furry legs were an endless expanse of strength against the pitch-black background. Every image was his beauty broken into parts, the components of perfect masculinity. They were more intimate than the Brassaïs or Mapplethorpes. It was beauty I had documented. I had loved and adored Aaron through the lens.

"Your father was upset by these images, Caleb. He asked me to talk with you about them." He reached down and took one of the photos in his hand.

"Yes, sir."

I didn't take my eyes from the photograph. I was angered by his touching it with his rough hands. It was a contrast in extreme, Aaron's youthful beauty juxtaposed against the doctor's aged decay. He pulled the photo close to his face as he examined the details through the top and bottom half of his bifocal lenses. I wanted to reach over and take the picture back. I hadn't made the pictures to entertain him. I'd made them for Aaron and me. I wanted to show Aaron how my eyes had seen him.

"I think that your father just doesn't understand them. Many people don't understand such photographs. Their own insecurity or lack of sexual maturity makes it hard for them to appreciate things of beauty. They lack the sophistication to see things clearly, Caleb. Do you understand?"

"I think so." I was still angered by his handling of my art.

"These are beautiful. You have a rare sight, Caleb. I can see how close you boys are in these pictures, but other people might not be able to see them the same way. I'm going to keep these for you. I will keep them safe and you can look at them here in my office anytime you want."

My heart broke at the thought of only being able to visit my beautiful photos. My shoulders dropped and I let a deep breath full of guilt and defeat pass through my lips.

"Would you like to pick just one to keep with you, Caleb?" The doctor sensed my sorrow. He offered a token gesture of one image for me to take with me, while he could keep and study all of my hard work anytime he wanted. He placed the photo he had picked up back on the desk.

I looked over the images. My eyes studied them all as quickly as I could. I lingered a few extra moments on the one the doctor had set back into place before I reached for it. It was the second one in the series: Aaron's full form, half in shadows and half in light. His face pointed straight at the camera, the tip of his nose was lit and his eyes were cast in shadow, while every contour of his body seemed to shine in the light. Though his eyes were obscured, I knew it was the shot taken when he looked directly through the lens and back into my eyes. It was a moment of complete trust. It was not a moment I was willing to let the doctor keep and scrutinize. I picked up the photo and held it close to my face, making careful note of every detail. I claimed that one to protect the moment we had shared.

"Aaron, would you like to keep one?"

He reached forward and took the first image in the series. It was the profile with the entire front of his body cast in shadow and the light breaking across his shoulders and down his back. The nape of his neck glowed like a beacon, the wild waves of his dark hair climbed across the frame and into darkness. A beautiful abstract that concealed his identity but also showed the perfection in his contours. Seeing it was like approaching a statue from behind, awestruck by the strength rendered in the curves and planes.

"If you boys take any more photographs like these, bring me the film and I'll have it developed for you. I know a place that handles artwork like this. They are most discreet." His crude hands gathered the photographs into a careless stack.

"We should tell your father that we talked of this. We should tell him that you understand that such things are inappropriate. He'll be happy with that answer. He lacks the sophistication to see it otherwise. Understood?"

"Yes," we chorused.

It was our last week at the day school and James Marshall was merciless. We were set to never see each other again, but James seemed determined to torture us enough that we would remember him all the way through our separate high school experiences. He taunted everyone with name-calling and threats. He promised to kick my ass before the year was through. I spent lunch in the shelter of the library and waited at the end of the day for half an hour before walking home to be certain the coast was clear.

It wasn't that I was afraid. I just didn't want the hassle. I didn't want to go home bloodied from a fight and then have to tell my father that I couldn't defend myself. I'd be left to admit that his own suspicions were shared by the school bastard, James Marshall. I didn't want to explain to my father that I had been beaten up by the class bully for being so different.

A bit queer.

A faggot.

Without anyone knowing about the art I made with Aaron, the same name my father had used had caught on at school. I tried to ignore it, but it infuriated Aaron.

Late in the week, I sat in the library during lunch and

heard a noise from the playground. The chanting of the other kids.

"Fight! Fight!"

Despite his widespread verbal attacks on my unpopular peers, I hadn't thought that James wanted to beat up anyone but me. Confused, I walked to the window and looked out at the playground. My heart sank to my stomach and my body ached with the force of panic.

I saw James Marshall huddled on the ground, terrified. His hands covered his face as the other kids cheered.

"Fight! Fight!"

Aaron was on his knees, with James locked between his legs at the waist. Aaron's closed fist struck the sides of his head, his chest, his shoulders, turning James into a bloodied mess. He was doing to James exactly what James had told everyone he would do to me before the year ended. I stuffed my books into my pack and ran out to the playground.

Aaron had left James behind and was walking briskly up the block away from the school. A few of our classmates were helping the bloodied James to his feet. I ran to catch up with Aaron.

"Aaron? Aaron!"

He walked quickly and crossed the street, ignoring my calls. His fists were still clenched at his sides.

"Aaron!" I finally caught up to him in the park two blocks from the school. "What happened?"

His breathing was heavy. His eyes wild. His cheeks soaked in tears, flushed with rage, he was trembling.

"He had it coming. He should have kept his mouth shut."

"What did he say? Aaron, what did he say?"

He wouldn't answer me. He just kept looking at me as he walked in circles and paced around me in the center of the park while he mumbled.

"I told him to shut the fuck up, he should've kept it shut, he should've shut the fuck up."

"What did he say?" Inside I was afraid I knew, but I needed him to tell me.

He stopped his pacing and stood facing me. Tears filled his eyes and his chest quaked with suppressed sobs. He wiped his nose on his sleeve and held his fists clenched.

"You're not a fag, okay! Nobody calls you that anymore! Nobody! You're not a fag." He fought to get the words out, and once they had been said he turned and ran away.

I stood silent. I didn't follow him.

My own eyes filled with tears.

I finished the last week of school alone. Aaron was expelled with only four days left in our last year at the day school. The cut-up and bruised James Marshall never said another word to me. He wouldn't even look in my direction. No one would.

James wasn't beaten for anything he said about Aaron. James had finally paid the price for the things he said about me. Aaron was sent away to visit his mother in New Jersey a week earlier than planned. Even though Chuck didn't pay Aaron any mind, he couldn't let a fight go without some kind of reprimand. It didn't feel like it was punishment for the fight, it felt like I was being punished for the feelings Aaron and I had for each other. I didn't get to say good-bye before Aaron was sent away and I wouldn't see or hear from him until after the summer passed, all because of what James had called me.

learning (adolescence)

After leaving the day school Aaron and I started our freshman year at the same high school on the advice of Dr. Moore. Our new school was the Walden Institute, on Eighteenth Street off Massachusetts Avenue, near Dupont Circle and a few blocks from the doctor's brownstone.

The institute was a college prep school designed for students who had problems in conventional high school settings. The classes were college level courses and scheduling was handled much like university life, with interdisiplinary studies where we were allowed to follow our interest. For some, the institute was the school of last resort, the place you ended up if you had ruined your chances everywhere else and your parents just wanted you to be ready to ship off to a decent college.

It reminded me of the island of misfit toys.

Unlike most of the other students, Aaron and I went directly from the day school to the institute without failing out of the conventional schools. Again we were different from the other kids. The doctor had advised our fathers that the institute was the best place for boys like us.

Within the first few days at the institute I became friends with a girl named Sonia. As soon as she saw me, she decided that I would make an interesting friend, and I didn't have much say in the matter. She loved to have interesting friends. She was only the second real friend I'd ever had. Aaron had always been my first and best friend.

Sonia was very different.

She was beautiful in a way that most women mature into. Her blond curls and stormy blue eyes were enhanced by her confidence and adventurous spirit. She could fit herself into any situation. With the other students she could be an icon of coolness and with their parents she could play the part of upstanding student. It wasn't that she was deliberately manipulative, she just managed to effortlessly adapt and present herself in the best light. She was a natural actress with keen insight into timing and place.

I'd seen her around the halls and she was in a couple of my classes: Comp and Modern Lit. Whenever Aaron and I milled around out front trying to decide where we wanted to go for lunch, Sonia would disappear down Eighteenth Street with a few of the institute's sketchier-looking boys. I'd noticed her but I hadn't given her any more thought than that casual observation.

If the institute had an "it" girl, she was Sonia.

She was the daughter of a prominent D.C. pediatrician and she lived in one of the few freestanding houses in Georgetown. It was a grand house in which her family had lavish parties and fund-raisers for museums. As the only child of one of Washington's elite, she led a privileged life. Her father was highly renowned and her mother was a striking socialite.

In spite of those advantages, Sonia was troubled. Her story was so much like the stories I'd read about Edie Sedgwick, with rumors of anorexia and drinking binges, that I was fascinated by her. She was the most complicated and the most beautiful girl I had ever seen. She was a superstar and I was intrigued by her.

Sonia was never friends with the other girls at the institute, only the boys.

Since Aaron and I were boys, Sonia simply picked one of us to talk to first.

"You live in Georgetown, too, huh?" Sonia asked me on the steps of the institute one afternoon.

I nodded a yes though I wasn't sure how to answer her question and get into a conversation. Having simple conversations with people troubled me. I had never felt I belonged around groups of people and my time at the day school had taught me to fear making a bad first impression. It was the first impressions that stuck and made me an outcast. She sensed something in my reply and, with a smile and raised eyebrow, proceeded with a one-sided conversation.

"Then you should walk me home now and then."

So we walked and got to know each other.

I didn't often have to say very much; Sonia took the lead with conversations. She always had something to talk about. Some days we walked straight to our houses in Georgetown. Some days we meandered through the streets looking in store windows. Sonia showed me how she thought I should dress and mocked the window displays along M Street and Wisconsin Avenue. Once a week we made a point of going to Swensen's so we could share a banana split, or we'd walk to Häagen-Dazs for coffee milkshakes. The split was always great, but Sonia liked to watch the boys behind the counter when we had our coffee shakes. The Georgetown Häagen-Dazs was ground zero for the punk rock boys in D.C. They kept mohawks and buzzed scalps hidden under their black ball caps. Sonia would stand at the counter long after ordering her shake and seductively sip through her straw as she made comments about what she'd love to do with the punk rock ice cream boys, always just loud enough to be overheard and make them smirk.

Sonia loved to watch the boys wherever we went. She said people-watching was her favorite hobby, but it was really the boys that she watched with the greatest enthusiasm. On Wednesdays we'd always go to watch Aaron at soccer practice. Sonia liked having a field full of boys to watch and she had opinions about each one, except Aaron. The only thing she said about him was a simple statement that held no meaning for me.

"He looks like Peter."

There were only about fifty students in our whole school and I didn't know any of them to be a Peter. I didn't think any of them looked like Aaron either.

"Who's Peter?"

"Oh, he went to the institute last year before you started. We kinda dated but there was some trouble and then he had to transfer out to Sandy Spring."

I didn't know where to go with those bits of information. Sandy Spring was a boarding school in Maryland. Anytime I seemed too difficult for my father and stepmother to deal with, boarding school was threatened. I'd heard of Sandy Spring. It was a Quaker school, hidden in the woods, just over the Maryland state line. I tried to remember if I'd heard anyone else at school mention Peter. I never talked to anyone other than Sonia and Aaron, but with a student body of less than fifty you didn't have to talk to that many people to know everything. The students of the institute enjoyed rumors, legends, and gossip more than any of their studies. Hardly anyone other than Sonia ever talked to Aaron and me but we'd still heard plenty about Sonia from the small handful of people that did speak to us. But I hadn't heard anything about Peter. And part of what she said I couldn't figure out on my own, so I pushed a little harder.

"Really? What does *kinda dated* mean?"

Sonia thought quietly as she watched the boys line up on the field. Aaron with his eyes locked on the ball, ready to take it from the offense. I waited and hoped that Sonia would answer me. Then Aaron took the ball and Sonia smiled.

"It's complicated. You see, I love Peter with all my heart and he loves me. We're a good pair and we understand each other. But, as much as Peter loves me, he . . . well, Peter can't really be in a relationship with a girl."

I thought through every word she said. I wasn't certain if I understood what she was saying. I didn't yet understand what *kinda dated* really meant. I didn't understand how Peter couldn't be in a relationship with a girl as beautiful as Sonia and I furrowed my brow trying to sort out the thoughts. She read my face and continued with her explanation.

"We tried. We fooled around plenty for him to know and he says he loves me. We're still the best of friends. He just isn't attracted to women at all."

The last part I understood. Perfectly.

"He's different. He likes guys?" I didn't know any of the nice words for it, just *fruit, fag, queer, fairy.* I'd heard them all, but none of those words seemed appropriate to our conversation.

"He's never been with a guy before. But yes. He thinks that's what he wants." Her eyes lit up as she watched the boys run along the grass. "Oh shit, our boy is going to make a goal!"

I looked from Sonia to the field as Aaron made the goal and we cheered him on. It was just a training scrimmage, not an actual game, but Aaron was still the hero on the field. He was always our sports star. I thought about what Sonia had just said about Peter, and I didn't know what to say about it.

Sonia seemed to understand it all pretty well. I understood how you could love someone and not be able to be with them because I'd felt that way about both of my friends. I felt like the thought of attraction or sex just seemed to complicate things with love.

"It's okay. I always seem to find the boys who aren't really attracted to me. But none of the other girls get to hang out with a better-looking bunch of them." With that she tucked her hand under my arm and laid her head on my shoulder. "He's good at soccer, and kinda pretty." She bobbed her head toward Aaron, on the field.

"Yeah. He always has been."

"You're a good friend, Caleb. To few, but you're the best."

"Thanks, you too." I kissed her head and watched Aaron strut back into his position on the lineup.

My father and stepmother were thrilled at the idea that Sonia might be my girlfriend. Sure, she was a complicated girl, but they thought having a girlfriend would finally straighten me out. They eagerly welcomed Sonia anytime she was around our house. My father would break from his stiff demeanor and go out of his way to appear charming. Sonia was everything my father approved of for me. She had social status, beauty, a wealthy family, and the appearance of being perfectly normal. Her company made me more tolerable to my family, and Sonia caught on to their approval right away and knew exactly how to play their game. Whenever my father was around she would make a point of showing her affection for me. She would hold my hand whenever we approached my father's house and give me a peck on my cheek whenever she left to go back to her house. And all while she coyly batted her eyes to make it appear that the affections were being snuck when she thought my father wasn't looking, though she knew that he was always looking. No matter where Sonia was, or who she was with, people always looked at her. She had charisma and star quality. She was always the center of attention.

"We should really get to work on those verbs, I have to get home for dinner soon." Sonia made the suggestion just loud enough to get my father's interest, but also to announce that we needed time alone to study. She had no intention of actually studying; French homework was just a cover for us to be left alone in the basement.

"Your mother speaks French, doesn't she?" my father asked as Sonia and I headed from the kitchen to the stairs.

"Yes sir, she lived in Paris for a few years before she met my father."

"Then you should know enough to help Caleb plenty with his verbs." For some odd reason all my father's small talk with Sonia sounded like innuendo. Innuendo that Sonia aptly played.

"Verbs . . . conjugations. The works, Monsieur Watson."

My father laughed as Sonia and I disappeared down the stairs.

"Your dad is pretty feisty. If he weren't your dad, I'd be tempted."

"He's friendly with you. He's kind of a jerk whenever anyone else is around. And come on, don't talk about doing my dad right in front of me."

"Are you and Aaron bisexual? It's okay, I'm bisexual. My mother says everyone was when she was modeling."

"Your mom was a model?"

"Yeah. Before I was born. In Paris. So, is Aaron your boyfriend?"

"We're just friends."

"But you love each other? You can see it."

"Come on. We're friends. Always have been. The kids back at the day school hated us both. All we had was each other. Just friends. Maybe more like brothers."

"Whatever you say, but it looks like you're fucking each other."

"We're best friends! Come on, Sonia. It's not like that."

She sorted through the Polaroids in the shoe box that she had pulled from my bookshelves.

"Are you sure you and Aaron aren't, you know?"

"Just friends."

"Well, you take a lot of Polaroids of your friend." She fanned a handful of photographs out and turned them toward me with a smirk on her face.

"Close friends." It was the only reply I could think of without having to explain anything further. What Aaron and I had was our collaboration. Aaron and I understood it as it happened, we just never talked about what our relationship might be outside of the art.

Sonia wasn't ever really crazy, she was just too honest for people. She never filtered anything, she just said whatever was on her mind and did as she pleased. It was easier for everyone to call her crazy than to deal with what she had to say or the impulses she acted upon. You could always count on her for the truth and for excitement. Whether it was something you wanted to hear or not was as unpredictable as she was.

night (stars)

It was a Sunday morning news program that introduced us to the creatures of the night. The story was about the culture surrounding screenings of *The Rocky Horror Picture Show* at the Key Theatre.

It was an exposé of water pistols, costumes, toast, and such.

None of this meant a thing to me at the time. I listened to the broadcaster's dull monotone, gibberish laid over video footage. But I was mesmerized by what I saw on the screen as I sat in the den eating my shredded wheat and my dad and stepmother slept off their fund-raiser hangovers upstairs.

Beautiful, colorful, androgynous half-naked people spending a late night just six blocks from my house. I watched them with my eyes struggling to make sense of everything I was seeing. They were amazing in the same way that a great painting or sculpture is amazing.

It was like a real-life Factory party was happening right down the street from my house. I had to find a way to meet them. My first thought was that I would need to sneak out and find them. While sneaking out of the house had gotten pretty easy since my parents were rarely concerned with my whereabouts anymore, they would never allow me to go out late at night to meet up with the creatures I saw on that screen.

As I was considering how I'd escape, the phone rang.

Sonia had watched the same clip on television and noted that the theater screened the film every night. She told me we were going and she'd meet me around the corner from my house at eleven thirty that night. She said it was best not to bring Aaron along as it wouldn't be his kind of thing. Then she abruptly hung up before I could say a word.

Her tone was very cloak-and-dagger.

Anticipation.

I was a ball of nervous energy that day, trying to prepare myself for the evening. Sonia and I had snuck out before but never with anywhere to go. For me, it wasn't even a matter of sneaking out anymore. My father had moved me into the basement apartment of the town house at my stepmother's request. They were expecting their first child and didn't want me to interfere once the little bundle of joy arrived. What was once my room had a wall knocked out of it to join it with the nanny's room and become a nursery suite. Having me in the basement with my own entrance gave them the illusion of being the perfect family. It was as though my father had a fresh start. The only thing that connected us was a door hidden in the coat closet on the ground floor of my father's home. A door my stepmother kept bolted shut after I moved the last of my things into the basement. Sonia could have just said she'd knock on my door at eleven thirty and it would have gone unnoticed, but it would have lacked the drama of meeting around the corner.

I had no idea how to dress for an evening of androgynous nighttime fun. I laid clothes out on the bed, trying to decide who I wanted to be. Should I wear a rep tie and an oxford with chinos? That choice seemed out of place. After I laid a dozen combinations on the bed I settled for just black: black Levi's, a black turtleneck, and my black windbreaker. It was my impersonation of casual studio Andy. Though I was dressed, I still had three hours to pass before I'd meet Sonia on the corner. I tried putting a bit of mousse in my hair and pushed it into a few styles, but then accepted that it wasn't going to help. I parted my hair on the side and combed it into place much in the same way I had in grade school. The effect I accomplished was that of an earlier Warhol. With all the attempts using mousse, I'd passed the hours failing at interesting hairstyles, so I grabbed my glasses and some cash out of my desk drawer and headed out to our meeting spot as Sonia had instructed.

I turned from the front gate of the town house and could see Sonia pacing back and forth under the streetlight. She, too, had decided to wear the all-black art school ensemble. Her version was a tight black miniskirt, mesh tank top, fishnets, biker boots, and a leather jacket. She looked a lot more like the characters on the news program than I. As I got closer to her I could see that she'd gone all out with the hair and makeup. Her blond curls were blow-dried to the wildest manelike extreme, her eyes rimmed in heavy kohl and her skin powdered to a theatrical porcelain. She had one of her mother's ridiculously long brown cigarettes burning between her fingertips and she puffed on it while furiously billowing clouds of smoke. Sonia never actually inhaled; she just puffed away at the cigarette, leaving behind thick clouds of smoke that would surround her like fog. For Sonia, smoking was just a prop.

"You look great, Sonia."

She really did look great. She was the perfect rock star. It wasn't the way she dressed for school. She'd made a quick study of the morning news program. She looked me up and down for a moment, then stepped forward and mussed my hair, pushing it forward into my eyes. She pulled my glasses off my face and stuck them in her bag as she rummaged about inside it, finally pulling out her kohl pencil.

"Hold still a minute, don't blink," she muttered, with the cap from the pencil grasped between her teeth.

She stepped forward and lined my eyes in the same manner she had made up her own. She took a moment to look from one eye to the other, just to be certain they were even. Once satisfied, she turned me around to look at my whole outfit. While my back was to her she tugged at the waist of my jeans, giving the denim a snug fit front and back. She turned me to face her again and smiled.

"You look good, too. You have any cash?"

Sonia never carried cash. That fact had turned into a running joke with Aaron and me. She was the daughter of one of the most prominent doctors in D.C. and she never seemed to have cash whenever we went out. It was so absurd we just had to laugh.

"Yeah, a bit." It was the same answer I always gave her. I didn't mind paying our way; it was great to have Sonia there for company. I don't think I would have had the nerve to go meet the creatures on my own. "Can I get my glasses back?"

"If you need them to see the movie. But right now your eyes look too cool, and you know that saying about making passes at guys in glasses. Let's go get our tickets."

"Hey, if we go down Prospect Street we can see the stairs."

"I don't want to see those stupid stairs. They freak me out." Sonia waved my suggestion off with her hand fanning at her clouds of smoke.

The stairs that freaked Sonia out were the same stairs that had been used in a famous horror movie set in Georgetown. It was the long tumble of stairs that could take you from Prospect down to M Street. They have always been one of my favorite spots in all of Georgetown and I couldn't get either Aaron or Sonia anywhere near them. It was just a movie. Actually, it was a movie and a book, but if you study the movie and visit the stairs the whole setup is pretty much impossible. There just didn't seem to be a way a priest could fly out a window and tumble down a stairway that runs perpendicular to how he would have flown out the window. Once I noticed that detail the stairs never scared me again. But there wasn't any convincing Sonia or Aaron of that, so Sonia and I walked down N Street to Wisconsin Avenue instead of visiting the stairs. As soon as we took the bend in Wisconsin at Prospect Street we had our first glimpse of the creatures in the flesh.

Sunday nights usually made Georgetown a ghost town, with the stores closed by five o'clock and the restaurants shuttered by ten. There were only a few bars that stayed open to draw the college crowd, but on a Sunday night even that was a rather bleak turnout. The sidewalk in front of the Key Theatre was the only hot spot. It was teeming with people. There were boys, girls, and some androgynous characters in between. All of them dressed in a punkish style made up of lingerie and leather. Sonia looked the part and fit right in with the crowd, while I considered turning around and going home. She sensed this and took hold of my hand. She leaned into my shoulder, like a girlfriend would.

"Isn't this cool"—more of an explanation than a question. She was determined that I stay and knew that her glee and excitement would keep me there. And I stayed, knowing we were having an adventure together. "Let's get our tickets and find some seats. I don't want to miss a thing!" She pulled me through the door to the ticket counter.

We walked through the doors and into the screening room. It was like we'd walked into the big top at a circus. The room was a dazzling world of color. Filled with a carnival of beauty, just like what we had seen outside on the curb. There was a flurry of activity near the screen. I squinted to see beautiful boys and girls in black leggings, vests, and tailcoats gathered there. Later we would learn that they were the Transylvanians, the ones who would dance the time warp. Though we didn't know the lingo then, we would learn everything about that world over the next few months. On our first night we were simply in awe of it. Neither of us could believe there was such color to the nightlife of Georgetown. I was overwhelmed with the sights of glitter and flesh. I tried to take as much in as I could. I tried to focus on what I saw, even though my glasses were hidden in Sonia's bag.

"I think I'm gonna need my glasses."

"When the movie starts. Let's sit somewhere in here." Sonia pulled me toward two seats right in the middle of the theater.

I looked around the room, amazed by the beauty all around us. It was androgynous beauty with all of its signals and clues mixed up. There was a kind of monotony to it that made me think of the Warhol paintings with their repeated image of a celebrity. The theater was filled with copies of the movie characters, with everyone wearing fishnets, corsets, satin, and leather. We had found a party like the ones I'd read about at the Factory. It was an inevitable plastic explosion happening just six blocks from my house. I was mesmerized by it.

The lights flashed on and off. When they did, the boys and girls in tailcoats scurried up and down the aisles, settling into whatever seats they could find.

"Are there any virgins tonight?" a red-haired girl in a golden tailcoat shouted from the center aisle.

Again, on that first night we didn't know all of the vocabulary, but I did know that neither of us were virgins. Sonia had helped me take care of that two months before the red-haired girl made the query.

Sonia had asked me if I'd ever had sex before and I had answered honestly. The answer was no, of course, so she made it her job to change that. We had sex three times in three days. Our first time was at her house after school. It was confusing and awkward for me. I had no idea what to do, and Sonia had to show me everything. It seemed like I couldn't get anything about sex right; I didn't even know what to do with my hands. She helped guide my erect cock into her, then I thrust up and down until I felt a shudder run through my body. I collapsed on top of her. The orgasm left me shocked and off balance. I don't think the first time did anything to satisfy Sonia, it was just an initiation for me.

The next two times we tried to fuck were at my house. Once you know the basics of what you're doing it should be easy to take it from there, but I would never say our next two attempts were any better than the first time. I still had trouble figuring out what to do with myself, and I had a hard time having an orgasm both times. I knew that my body was in working order, but I felt like I couldn't concentrate. I liked

Sonia, but I didn't desire her. Whenever I looked into her eyes, she looked like she just wanted it to be over. I tried to think of the feeling of my first orgasm with her and quickened my thrusting in and out until I had another one. Then instead of collapsing on top of her, I rolled onto my back and lay beside her. It was after our third afternoon of sex that Sonia decided that since the deed had been done three times I wasn't a virgin anymore. We agreed we shouldn't keep screwing each other since we were best friends. She didn't think we had the right chemistry together. I thought I had no chemistry at all. I wondered why people made such a big deal out of sex. Doing it felt awkward to me and I didn't enjoy anything about it, not even the brief orgasm. Afterward the subject of sex didn't come up again for a month. When it finally did, it was a brief conversation. Sonia said she had had a problem "taken care of," and I didn't understand what she meant at first. Then she said it had been a little problem. I understood that. She never told me how it had been taken care of or where. Just that it had been taken care of. I knew then that we couldn't have really taken care of a little problem on our own. I was relieved that we didn't have to, though I often wondered what our little problem might have looked like.

The girl in the golden tailcoat caused me to remember our little problem. I sank into my seat to avoid her question. I tried to put my answer out of my mind. I stared forward blankly at the screen as the houselights went dark and the crowd began to cheer. Sonia handed me my glasses and settled next to me without a word. I think she must have remembered our little problem, too.

The red curtain opened to reveal a pair of bright red lips that sang a tune over the opening credits on the screen. The crowd started to go wild, singing along and talking to the screen. I glanced over at Sonia, and she was already enthralled by what she saw, her eyes dashing from the screen to all of the regulars at the front of the theater. It was just too much to comprehend on that first night. My mind was overrun by the film, the audience participation, and the props that everyone had brought. During the first half hour of the film the room was chaos, but rehearsed chaos with everyone playing a part. The Transylvanians time-warped on the screen and in the theater. I watched every bit of the movie being re-created by the audience. The spectacle of it moved Sonia to the edge of her seat as I remained slouched into mine, trying to take in the details. As the vibrancy of the floor show spilled from the screen into the theater I began to understand what I was watching. It was the energy of night, glamour, glitter, color, and decadence. It was a raw expression of acceptance.

Suddenly the source of all the excitement appeared on the screen and the floor. It was the superstar's entrance and he was the sweet transvestite from Transsexual Transylvania: Frank N. Furter. He was the most beautiful one of them all, and we were graced with his presence on the screen and with a meticulous copy in the theater. It was an icon in duplicate. With a smirk on his garnet lips he invited us all up to the lab to see what was on the slab.

I looked at Sonia. She was slack-jawed in amazement. She looked back at me and a smile spread across her face. She silently mouthed the words *fucking awesome.* That night we recognized that we had found a place that felt like home.

After the show we sat on the curb outside the theater and watched everyone leave. Sonia puffed away on one of her cigarettes as she waved her hands in the air. She gestured wildly as she told me everything that had happened, as though I hadn't been next to her all along. I stared forward at Wisconsin Avenue and nodded as I listened to her story. She hadn't missed a thing. She had every nuanced detail of the story and audience participation committed to memory from one viewing. Her excitement was electric. I took her cigarette out of her flying hand and took a deep hard drag off of it before I offered it back to her.

"Nah, finish it. . . ." She continued with the moment-by-moment recap as I inhaled another deep drag of smoke, exhaling through my nose and smiling as my friend told me an excitedly vivid tale of our night.

"Well, what do we have here, a couple of little superstars?"

I heard a voice coming in our direction and each word in the question was punctuated by the click of high heels on concrete. I looked over my shoulder to see the Transylvanian as she approached us. She was wearing a tailcoat, fishnets, and stilettos, just like the others. But this one was a young blond girl who looked like Marilyn Monroe. Sonia was silenced by the approach, slack-jawed again. I stood and turned to greet the blond starlet.

"Hi, I'm Caleb." I offered my hand and the starlet placed her velvet glove there for a kiss.

"Darlin', that name is just too biblical to come out of this mouth." She reached up and tousled my hair. "But you look just like a little Andy Warhol. So I think that's what I'll call you. Okay, Andy baby?"

Sonia laughed at the nickname.

"Perfect," she purred as she stood next to me.

"And who is this little superstar? Certainly a socialite or a debutante? Your Edie?" The starlet looked Sonia up and down as she questioned me coyly.

"Um . . . eh . . . this is Sonia," I nervously introduced Sonia to the starlet.

"A pleasure to meet you, darlin'. I'm Brit."

The starlet had a name.

"And you obviously already know my friend Andy. Are the two of you . . . intimately acquainted?" Brit asked with a slight arch of her brow.

Before I could get a word out Sonia responded.

"We were. But that didn't really work for us."

"Then you won't have to be jealous when Miss Brit steals Andy away, will you, darlin'?" With that Brit slid her gloved hand into the bend of my elbow.

Sonia smirked and took up a mirroring position at my other side.

"There's no reason to steal. We can always share."

"What a clever girl you have there, Andy. She's gonna go far. I'm famished. Are you kids hungry?"

"Sure." I looked at Sonia, who nodded a yes as well. "Where should we go?"

"Well, all the kiddies from the show go up to Au Pied. It's fabulous. And where else can we get lobsters at this hour, anyway? You'll love it, Andy!" With that, Brit started to lead us up Wisconsin Avenue.

Au Pied was Au Pied de Cochon, a French dining hall I'd been to many times with my family. It had rooms in the classic style of wood panels with a zinc bar and crisp linens. I'd been there for brunches and lunches on most weekends over the years and it had great atmosphere, but I'd always found it a bit stuffy. By day it was host to the most conservative side of Washington. It was with Sonia and Brit that I discovered Au Pied had another face at night.

Once we were inside the doors it felt as though we had discovered a new world. It was not the same as it had been on any visit with my family. The rooms were filled with the loud rumblings of conversation, smoke, music, and the glittery creatures of the night. It was like the stories I'd read of the famed Max's Kansas City and Warholian parties that took place there. Our new friend had walked us through the doors into a dream of glitter and shadows. We were in a place that was nothing like the world I lived in. It all felt like home to me, and when I looked over at Sonia her eyes beamed with pure pleasure for what we had found that night.

"Come on, kids, we sit in the back."

Brit started to weave her way through the main room, walking past the bar and into a back room with dim lights, black leather banquettes, red lacquered walls, and vintage cigarette posters. Brit moved through the room like a true starlet. She was Andy's Marilyn, in all her brilliant glory. Floating across the dark wood floors on her stilettos, she flirted with the admirers along her path to the round banquette in the corner. It was the grandest table in the dining hall, the table that would be center stage if it were a theater. When we arrived, several of the gang from the theater stood to allow Brit to slide into her seat next to the sweet transvestite. She had led us right to him; we were sitting at the table with Frank. She kissed his cheek and patted her hand on the seat, motioning for Sonia and me to join them. I scooted into place next to Brit, followed by Sonia.

"Everyone, this is Andy and his little socialite Sonia. Andy, this is everyone." Brit motioned to the crowded table with her gloved hand and we were greeted with a chorus of *hello*s and *hey*s.

"Andy and Sonia were lovers, but Sonia's willing to share." Brit declared this shared secret to her audience as the waiter handed menus to all the new arrivals.

Sonia laughed at the comment and she started looking over the menu as she leaned over to whisper a question in my ear.

"You have some cash, right?"

I nodded as Brit started to whisper in my other ear. She

introduced me to Frank, whose real name was Robbie. I looked past her to Robbie's smiling lips as Brit warned me of one last thing.

"Watch out for Robbie. He likes the arty boys like you, Andy. He and I have an off-and-on thing. But he really likes boys like you."

The three of us ordered lobsters and every time I glanced past Brit I could see Robbie watching my every move.

After that first night Sonia and I rarely missed a showing of *Rocky Horror* at the Key Theatre. We had been taken under Brit's wing and learned everything we could about nightlife.

Brit was a true starlet, the kind of girl people call a living legend. She was always immaculate with her hair and makeup. She would wear great vintage party dresses from the junk shops like they were the finest couture. If Audrey Hepburn's Holly Golightly had been a cool punk rocker, she would have been Brit. She lived like a superstar and without any apologies for it. Anything that didn't satisfy or please Brit right away was changed. She loaned Sonia the right outfits for going out, she instructed me on what she thought I should wear, and she even changed my name because it didn't suit her whims. In Brit's world I was always Andy.

After we'd spent a couple of weeks with the starlet I asked Sonia if we could invite Aaron along to see the show. I wanted to share our new experiences with him. I needed to share with him the decadent world we had discovered.

"Go ahead. But he better not mess it up."

I never understood what she meant by that comment. I didn't recall Aaron ever messing anything up for us. He wasn't so different from me in his shyness. I never thought he wasn't cool or anything like that. Sonia's comment seemed out of place.

"Why don't you ask Peter to come along, too?"

"No. That would certainly mess things up. Peter's entirely too straitlaced to join us at the circus. Anyway, the last thing I need is for Pete to meet up with you and the boy wonder."

I asked Aaron to go out with us on a Friday night. I was excited to share the creatures, the night, Au Pied, and everything else with him. I couldn't wait for him to meet Brit and all of our new friends. But more than anything, I wanted him to see how accepting their world was.

Sonia and I both forgot to mention the initiation of the virgins. When the girl in the golden tailcoat called for the virgins neither of us was quick enough to catch Aaron before he headed to the front of the theater. Sonia looked over scowlingly and I shrugged. We sank down in our seats. I hoped that the initiation would be over as quickly as possible and that Aaron would have a sense of humor about it.

Somehow Sonia and I had never been subjected to the traditional virgin experience of *The Rocky Horror Picture Show*. It was a good-hearted prank the regulars enjoyed playing on the newbies. If anyone was naive enough to stroll to the front of the theater when asked, they were then subjected to a bit of public humiliation known as the initiation of the virgins. The experience was a shock treatment for your inhibitions.

Sonia and I had seen the initiation played out many times before. We would've never imagined that Aaron would bolt out of his seat and to the front of the room without asking us if he should. Sonia shaded her eyes and stared at the palm of her hand while I squirmed in my seat. I could see the girl in the golden outfit as she told the newbies what the plan was and what they had agreed to. Aaron glanced back toward our seats and his brows knit themselves into the puzzled look I knew well. It was the look Aaron would give me when the next words out of his mouth were going to be *You kidding me?* It was his strong New Jersey accent that made those words into a moment like the best slapstick comedy.

"Oh shit, he's gonna do it." Sonia sat up in her seat and glanced over at me with a cheerful smirk beaming across her face.

I could see Brit as she marched up the center aisle. She leaned into our row and laid her velvet-gloved hand on the back of the seat next to me. Her ruby glossed smile had questions.

"He's the notorious Aaron I've heard so much about?"

"Yeah." I shifted in my seat and she took Aaron's empty seat.

"That one certainly knows how to make a first impression, huh, Andy?"

I kept my mouth shut and hoped it would end as soon as possible. I was ready for the floor show to start. Once that scene was finished I knew Aaron would be released by the Transylvanians and he'd be free to find his way back to our row, perhaps without wanting to kill us all.

"Aren't you going to go help them?"

"Oh no, Andy, Miss Brit wants to see this one from the floor." The starlet patted my knee as she settled in to watch an initiation, instead of participate in it as she usually did.

The film started to play and the regulars played out their parts. As the initiation moment approached I became more restless. I didn't want it to go badly for Aaron. I was afraid he'd hate me for not preparing him for it. I stirred in my seat as the first twenty minutes of the film played out, unable to figure out what Aaron was thinking about the chaos around him.

The initiation at the Key Theatre screenings of *Rocky Horror* always took place during the lab scene. Brad and Janet are invited up to the lab to see what's on the slab and then they are promptly stripped down in front of the rest of the cast. Life imitates art as the Transylvanians get them out of their wet traveling clothes. For the floor show in the theater this was the perfect initiation for newbies. It gave the regulars a chance to publicly humiliate the virgins, and it's hard to keep too many inhibitions to yourself when you're standing in front of a roomful of strangers while wearing just your underwear. Sonia and I had both gotten off the hook with the initiation, but no one ever seemed to get wise to that. And by the time it would have come up we were regarded as regulars.

Aaron stood at the front of the theater and watched the beginning of the film on the screen. I could see him as he regarded the floor show around him with a look of amused curiosity. Doing just as they always did when the movie reached the fateful scene, the Transylvanians began the initiation. When they did, Aaron looked them over with a smirk on his face while they stripped him down to his briefs. I was relieved that it appeared he had a sense of humor about it.

Aaron never hid his body, but he didn't flaunt it either. Soccer and genetics kept him naturally fit. His dark good looks were coupled with a naive lack of awareness of them. He was shy, but never bashful. He laughed as the Transylvanians undressed him. It wasn't a nervous laugh. It was a true one—he was ticklish. Though his style of beauty seemed out of place among the others in front of the screen, Aaron had become the star of the night by the time his trousers were off. His young, chiseled, athletic physique earned him double takes all around.

As I studied his silhouette against the screen I felt pride. I was proud of him for his courage and beauty, which was seen by everyone in the theater that night. He was my best friend and for so long he'd been the only friend I had ever known.

Aaron's beauty disrupted things that night. The cast had trouble following along with the floor show because they were stealing glances at the beautiful boy who stood gazing at the screen. Brit sensed this would upset Robbie and she made her move.

"Well, well, well, darlings, Miss Brit should go try to save the day. I'll send your boy back to you in just a sec."

Brit walked down the aisle to the screen. She parted the crowd of Transylvanians as she picked up Aaron's jeans and T-shirt from the floor and handed them back to him. The initiation was over and Robbie needed the limelight back. Aaron nodded and looked toward our row. He pulled his jeans up over his briefs, then tugged his T-shirt over his head as he walked up the aisle. Everyone in the theater watched him take his seat back with Sonia and me.

"Good job, kiddo," Sonia congratulated him as he sat down.

"You guys never told me about the initiation."

Sonia and I exchanged looks and thought it better not to tell him that we had never been initiated. We didn't want to explain to Aaron why it was that the virgin question had tripped us up. We'd never told Aaron about the three afternoons that were my answer to the other question about virginity. Those days after school had been my initiation.

"I met your friend Brit. She seems nice. She told me to ask you guys if we were going to breakfast." Aaron scrunched his brows, the way he always did, as he squirmed around in his seat and tucked his shirt back into his jeans.

"Yeah, breakfast is fun."

"Hey. Do either of you have any cash?" Sonia leaned over to ask.

We nodded and laughed at the question we had started to think of as Sonia's trademark.

"Yeah, we've got it," we answered in unison. Which made us laugh more.

On his first night at *The Rocky Horror Picture Show,* Aaron had survived with his humor intact.

collaboration (art)

I began making my films after we started going to *The Rocky Horror Picture Show*. My first movie camera was a Bell + Howell Focus-Matic XL 8mm silent model that I'd bought from the Best Company store on Wisconsin Avenue. The film came in cartridges that I could send away in a mailer. I experimented with making stop-motion animations on a chalkboard. These were silly stick-figure animations that were tedious to make. I wasn't happy spending hours drawing stick figures to have just two minutes of film. I grew frustrated with the process and the camera ended up being retired to a bookshelf with a stack of comics. Without the right subjects I was ready to abandon my film career.

One afternoon in my room Brit stumbled across my movie camera and grew excited by the discovery. She'd seen a few art films with me at the Hirshhorn and her find gave her ideas.

"Andy, why don't you make a few movies? You already have a cast. Your own little Edie and Gerard." She held the viewfinder to her eye and panned the lens across my bedroom as she told me of the brilliant plan she had in mind. "You could shoot 'em right here in your room." She lowered the camera from her face and engaged me with her widened gaze. Having made her idea both a question and an exclamation, she let her free hand rest on her hip and awaited my answer.

"I don't know anything about making movies. You have to figure out lights, scripts, directing stuff," I said as I shrugged at her suggestion.

"Darlin', I've been to those films with you. Take the shades off your lamps and point the camera. The debutante and the boy wonder can figure the rest out. I'll be your assistant director. You'll see." She had made the confident declaration and she started to spin herself around in my desk chair.

Brit was always certain of things. The only exception to that boldness was her habit of quietly tapping on my windows whenever she came over. I had my own entrance to the base-ment apartment of my father's town house, and he was rarely around, but Brit was still cautious anytime she came over. I never made a big deal out of this break in her character. I figured the seventeen-year-old starlet would be a little hard to explain to my parents anyway.

I started our project with black-and-white film. Doing so made it easier for me to get the lighting right and hold the sharp contrast tones I liked to see on the screen. Shooting my movies in this way made them look like Warhol's early film works, with their grainy footage, stark lighting, and only the sound of the projector as the score. We watched our first movies in the darkened basement together. I was making new art and living art as Aaron, Brit, and Sonia became my superstars. We made four films together, three of them inspired by Andy Warhol productions and one that was an original concept.

Sleep was the first film that I made. It didn't include my whole cast of superstars. It was an experiment in using film to document my way of seeing things in my world. I shot it on a night that Aaron stayed at my apartment. Earlier in the week I had purchased a pack of film cartridges with the intention of starting up the Factory-like studio that Brit had suggested. After Aaron had fallen asleep on my bed, I watched him, and then remembered reading something about a night when Warhol filmed a friend of his as the friend slept. It was one of Andy's first movies.

I quietly pulled the camera from my bookshelf and made the necessary adjustments for the low lighting in my apartment. Then I carefully loaded the film cartridge into the camera and tried to close it without making any noise. I didn't want to wake Aaron. I sat next to the bed and started the film rolling with the press of the trigger. I panned the lens along Aaron's body and traced the contours of it as I listened to the reel wind along inside the camera. I was careful not to wake him while I studied him through the viewfinder. I filled the first cartridge with my travels from his legs up to his jaw. At times I lingered on some parts, but then I would resume my travel as I passed the lens along the landscape created by his dark hair and caramel-golden skin. I loaded a second cartridge into the camera and sat quietly on the floor next to the bed as I continued filming. On the second reel I captured a steady shot that showed his slightest movements and how his breath stirred him as he slept. It was in those moments that I learned how to see through the lens in a new way. Just as with photography, I taught myself to be a filmmaker with the lessons that I learned on Aaron's body. I wanted to give the things I had seen on our still images movement and breath.

A good film can freeze moments and preserve them. A great film can capture feelings. It was like a writer rendering beauty with a poem.

Everything changed with that film. I started to understand the feelings I was having as I watched Aaron sleep through the lens. It was as though love transmitted through the camera in front of my face. I'd never felt as awake as I did filming him that night.

My initial attraction to him had become something else and my heart recognized it as something warmer and softer than I had previously known. I felt as though my gaze had shifted a bit. I was refining my perspective. I realized that what was a curiosity to me had become essential. More than ever before, I saw that he possessed magnificent beauty and in his slumber I could see his truths. I saw the things that captivated my heart in an honest form. Asleep he had no artifice, pretense, or any of the shields that he put up by day. Having gently traced the contours of his face with the lens I felt I understood more of him. I had studied every detail through the viewfinder by the dim city lights at two in the morning and found myself captivated. It was as though I filmed a daydream and the camera captured the moments, hours, days of yearning. The image on the film was both the subject and object of my desire. It was Aaron sleeping and at peace. I felt a sense of suspended contentment and I wanted to hold Aaron in our contentment forever. It seemed that I could protect him from his troubles and preserve that with the film. If I suspended the moments with film would I stop seeing him as he struggled through our adolescence? Would my movie make his youthful beauty immortal or would he be more beautiful as he became a man in the waking world?

I filled five cartridges that night. With the last one I let the frame rest on the plane of his neck in the spot where his jaw had started to become more masculine and solid than before. It was here that his beard had become denser and created a shadow. In the center of the frame I focused on the indentation made by the clavicle before it travels beneath the muscles of the shoulder. I captured a landscape of breathtaking beauty on the black-and-white film. I'd made three solid minutes of one part of his body my abstract image rendered in gray scale. Once the movie was projected it could be read as a map that led to where I most wanted to be. I watched through the lens and wanted to stop in that spot. I wanted to rest my lips in that hollow between neck and shoulder, inhale the scent that emanated from it and drift into sleep myself. The raw intensity of these thoughts swarmed in my head as I heard the reel inside the camera click to a stop. With the last of the five cartridges finished, I set the camera down and continued to watch him sleep. I scanned my eyes up and down my subject. I knew that I loved him. I loved him as a friend, a muse, and as a brother. I had no context for how much I loved Aaron. I'd never loved anyone before. I didn't even know what the feelings I had really meant, I just knew that I had them.

The next day I sent the five cartridges away in a mailer and a few weeks later they were returned as developed reels. I didn't sort them into any kind of order as I spliced them together and wound them onto an empty projection reel. I even left the white headers on the end of each strip as I wound it to the larger reel. With the five cartridges of film attached to one another I had made a fifteen-minute film when it was played at its standard speed. But, in imitation of Warhol, I adjusted the projector to slow it to half-speed as I'd read he had done with the films *Sleep* and *Kiss*. This projection trick gave our landscape of sleep a running time of a half hour.

I kept the film a secret, even from Aaron. I watched it alone in my room a few times until I felt certain that I had every beautiful detail committed to memory. Only then did

I share it with him in the darkened basement of my father's town house.

The room was silent except for the hum of the projector and dark but for the light on the screen. We sat next to each other and let the film play through the half-hour version. Aaron never took his eyes from the screen. When the film strip finished its trip through the projector I reached over and flipped the switch, leaving the room dark. In that darkness neither of us said anything. I felt Aaron's weight shift next to me and then I felt his lips on my own as he gave me a gentle kiss. I could feel his warm breath in front of me as he lingered a moment after the kiss, and then I heard his voice.

"Thank you for letting me watch this," he whispered to me before he walked out and left me sitting alone in my room.

I sat on the edge of my bed and tried to hold on to the smell of him that lingered in front of me. It was the scent of his green striped soap and I never wanted it to fade away from me.

I never screened that film for anyone else but Aaron. He watched it only once and we never talked about *Sleep* past that night when he thanked me with a kiss.

Blow Job was the first film that I made with my entire cast of superstars, and it was the one film that was a direct copy of the Warhol original that inspired it. Though it involved my full cast of friends, only Aaron appeared on-screen. I hadn't seen the original, but it was often mentioned in books about

Warhol and his movies. The original was made with a continuous shot of only the actor's face and shoulders in frame as he received a blow job from a person or persons who were never seen by the audience.

Sonia and Aaron were nervous on the day we filmed *Blow Job,* while Brit made jokes about embarking on a grand new career of pornographic narration. She imagined herself becoming the Marlin Perkins of erotica, *Wild Kingdom* of the flesh, even though I made it clear that we were recording without an accompanying audio track.

All of my superstars thought the film would be possible to make when I described it, but there was a bit of tension nonetheless. We agreed that as close friends, nothing about filming should be complicated. It was another experiment. It was an art project.

Sonia brought a bottle of wine she'd stolen from her parents' collection, and my actors took turns drinking straight from the bottle to loosen themselves up for their roles. I had picked up extra film, set the camera on a tripod, and marked out space on the wall to show them all the parts of the shot that would be in frame. When they finished the bottle of wine, I went over the concept one last time and everyone nodded that they understood it. Just as in the original, I assured everyone that it would never be clear who performed the act and that the camera would be documenting only the effects. We all agreed that was an important part of the film's concept. Though he was relaxed from the wine, Aaron was still a bit hesitant. Brit and I had costumed him as close as possible to the still photos we'd seen of the original film by dressing him in a black T-shirt with a black leather jacket over it. The only part that could be seen through the viewfinder was the up-turned collar of the jacket and his head.

Aaron stood in place with his back to the wall in the spot I had marked out for him so that I could adjust the lighting. I took a few Polaroids and used them to check the setup on the peel-apart film while the girls touched up their makeup, even though neither of them would appear in a single shot. I showed Aaron the Polaroid proofs and asked him if he was ready to start. His eyes darted around the room nervously before he made eye contact with me.

"Yes." He said it quietly in the brief moment he met my eyes before he turned his gaze to the floor.

"Okay. Just relax and be natural. Don't worry about anything. We have plenty of film. Don't worry if I have to change cartridges, just keep everything going naturally." I tried to direct the shot before I started. "Don't try to fake it because this works only if it screens as real. If this gets too weird for you we can stop. Just tell me you want to stop. Okay?"

Aaron nodded his head again to say that he understood, and he was ready to make our second film together. I reached forward and turned the collar of his jacket up. I smiled at him as I stood behind the camera and looked the scene over as the girls moved into their places. I took one last look through the viewfinder to check the shot before we started. I stepped forward and moved Aaron over a couple of inches so that his face would be in the center of the shot with the light hitting him hard from the right. This placed the left side of his face in shadows. I took two steps back and asked him if he needed a minute to get himself ready. He nodded as he unbuttoned his jeans and slid his hand into the waistband of his white briefs. I took my place on the other side of the viewfinder and watched him. Through the lens I looked him in the eye and silently questioned if he was ready to start. As though he could intuit my thoughts, he nodded another yes. Then I pulled the trigger on the camera and gave my superstars their cue to begin.

"Remember. Art is what you can get away with. Action!"

The room was silent. I could hear the film rolling in the camera and it was all that I listened to, so I didn't hear either Brit or Sonia. I didn't see anything outside the frame I had set for the shot as I smoothly changed film cartridges without ever looking away from the viewfinder. I never took my eyes off Aaron's face.

In the beginning he seemed self-conscious, with his eyes darting around the room. He looked down at the floor every few moments and then he'd tilt his head back to look at the ceiling. It was after I loaded the second cartridge that he seemed to relax. He closed his eyes from time to time and he opened them only to look through the lens and into my eyes as I filmed him. I could see when his breathing got harder and quickened as his eyes glazed with a look of euphoric pleasure. The whole time I watched him his eyes would open and look back at me through the camera and his focus would sharpen again. He teased me as he brought himself to the brink of release and fought to hold it all back by refocusing himself. He maintained that level of control through another two cartridges of film. When I loaded the last cartridge and looked through the viewfinder I sensed he was questioning me with the look in his eyes. It was as though he asked me if I was ready for him to finish the act.

"Yes. If you can."

His head tilted forward and his body shuddered with the first pulse of pleasure. It was with the second pulse that he drew in a deep breath and slammed his head back against the wall. Then his jaw slackened and he took a few shallow but heavy breaths before a third pulse shot though his body. With that his head tilted down and his eyes closed as he bit into his bottom lip and let out a soft whimpering sound followed by a muffled moan. His shoulders shrugged and twitched with the last pulse of pleasure, and with an exhale of breath through his nose he opened his eyes and looked directly into the lens of the camera. He looked there because he knew I hadn't missed a moment of what he'd done.

I pressed the trigger to stop the film and I remained there as I studied his face through the viewfinder. He stood with his eyes locked onto the lens, though he knew the film had stopped rolling. I watched him while my mind sped through my memory of what I had seen. I considered the intensity of his expression and the great spectrum of emotions that had played out with the act of a blow job that I hadn't actually witnessed. I had not seen anything below Aaron's collar as

I watched him perform a play of shyness, fear, agony, and pleasure. He had held my gaze and engaged me with his eyes through the entire thing and it was as though we had been the only two people in the room. My mind raced to understand the meaning of such an exchange.

"Darlin', you're a great actor!"

Brit's exclamation broke the silence of the tense moment. The girls giggled as I looked up from the viewfinder at the two of them as they wandered away from Aaron. He buttoned his jeans and looked away from the camera before he crossed the room to check the wine bottle. He shook it gently to be certain it was empty.

I sent the cartridges away to be developed and received the processed film a few weeks later. Once I had spliced the reels together I had the superstars over for a screening. We sat in my apartment and watched the movie together. No one ever told me who had performed most of the act and I never asked who had given the blow job. It was the film I had wanted to make and that was all that mattered to me.

After the screening nothing about that film was ever mentioned again. Sonia said it was the most raw emotion she had ever seen, and Brit said she didn't realize Aaron could say so much with his silence. Aaron kept that silence through the screening. His only comment about our second film together was in a whisper as he hugged me on his way out the door to go home on the night of the screening.

"You make good films."

Kitchen was the only film we made with sound. My father had given me a Betamax camera and we made our third film with it. It was our first experiment with videotape and sound.

The premise of *Kitchen* was simple enough. Sonia and Brit played two girlfriends sitting around the kitchen table drinking coffee and chatting. They complained about their hectic lives and their worthless boyfriends as they chatted about all the girly things: cramps, abortions, and shopping.

Sonia had blown her blond curls into a wild shaggy mane and she had taken to wearing vintage foundation garments with men's trousers in a style she had adapted from Madonna's videos on MTV. Brit had shown up that day with a whole new look herself. She'd changed her platinum bob into a blackened hot curler set and she wore a black vintage cocktail dress. She had morphed from Marilyn Monroe into Sophia Loren. I didn't ask any questions about it as I figured it might read better on the film. The contrast between the girls played out to represent that all women had the same problems with men no matter what they looked like. I didn't mind if the superstars changed themselves as long as the changes made good film.

The girls took their places at the table and I started the videotape. The red light on the front of the camera glowed and I motioned with my hand that the girls could start talking as the tape had started to record. Aaron's role in the film was to wander in and out of the shot as he played the role of Sonia's boyfriend. He entered the scene in only his tight white briefs and crossed over to the refrigerator to drink milk straight from the carton with drops of it dripping from the corners of his mouth onto his chest and eventually dampening the front of his briefs. This first appearance of Aaron as the boyfriend set the girls off to spend five minutes in shared grief about what pigs men are. He stood proudly in his briefs, the emblem of Everyman, as he took the abuse from the women. His pride was justified by his body, which soccer had made lean and solid. The girls had a hard time playing their parts without stealing glances at Aaron in all his glory.

The video camera allowed for our film to be made as one continuous shot, without the rough breaks that changing out cartridges in the movie camera had produced. Unfortunately, this left us with what might have been called lots of dead air. When things started to drag I would try to prompt things by making some comment from off camera. I asked Brit to talk about her boyfriend Robbie and she spent a few minutes speaking about anal sex in a most animated fashion. She complained that on all fours looking away was the only way she could keep Robbie interested in her.

"But I'm sure he'd trade my ass for this one any day!" Brit cackled with laughter as she leaned forward and slapped Aaron's cotton-clad butt.

Aaron crossed in front of the table and stood next to Sonia so that he was out of Brit's reach. He didn't know how to respond to the slap, even though his briefs started to show more of a bulge. He leaned down and gave Sonia a kiss. It was a stage kiss without any feeling. A blank kiss just to resolve the bulge. When he pulled away from her, Sonia slapped him across his face and then she spit on the floor.

I pressed the red button to stop the tape and placed the cap over the lens. *Kitchen* was the last film we made on videotape. It had a complex story in the end but I didn't like the quality of videotape. Missing the sharp contrast and tones of black-and-white film, it didn't feel like art and it lacked the beauty I could make with the 8mm camera. But Aaron's appearance in his briefs saved the entire project from being ugly to me.

After we'd filmed *Kitchen,* Brit stood at the sink in my bathroom and touched up her makeup. She meticulously layered garnet-red cream onto her lips and penciled in perfect Elizabeth Taylor eyebrows. Aaron tugged on his jeans in the corner. Sonia and I watched as my superstars came back to themselves. They left the film fantasy behind and put their reality costumes back on. Sonia sat on the corner of the bed while I swiveled in my desk chair and watched Brit as she painted her face. With a smirk, I asked the question that had been demanding an answer.

"So Brit, what's with the hair?"

"Oh, you noticed?" Brit shot a glance toward me as she pulled a tissue up to blot her lips before she added another layer of garnet. "Robbie had to go home to Indiana for some family drama, so the kiddies asked me to play Frank while he's gone." She blotted her lips for yet another layer.

"But Frank is a guy?"

Aaron's statement was also a question that hung awkwardly in the room. It made the air thick and caused the rest of us to exchange a series of puzzled looks. None of us knew quite how to respond to his query. Sonia let out an unguarded snort of a laugh but then stopped herself short.

"Thank you, darlin'," Brit responded, with a touch of hesitation, as she looked at Aaron and tried to gauge the sincerity of his remark.

There was nothing but silence as Brit, Sonia, and I exchanged glances.

"Well, how are ya gonna work that out?" Aaron's question was heartfelt as he pulled his T-shirt over his head.

It had never occurred to me that he didn't know about Brit, and the girls were just as stunned as I was by his question. The looks we exchanged told us all that one of us should say something. We had to clear the matter up.

"Darlin', come here. Momma has to talk to you privately." Brit motioned for Aaron to join her in the bathroom.

Once they were inside and he was sitting on the closed toilet seat, Brit turned and held a finger in the air to Sonia and me. It was her signal that she would be just a minute. Then she closed the door and Sonia and I looked at each other with stunned faces.

Sonia mouthed the words *He doesn't know?*

I shrugged. We both covered our mouths with our hands to keep from bursting into laughter. A few moments passed silently as the two of us tried to guess what Brit might say to explain things to Aaron. We didn't imagine that she would actually show him anything.

"WHOA!" Aaron's shocked response to Brit's decision to play show and tell caused Sonia to snicker into a pillow.

"Shit." I looked at Sonia as she held the edge of the pillow to her face. I'd let my reaction out in a hushed tone with extra emphasis on the *shhhh*.

The door to the bathroom swung open. Aaron sat there stunned while Brit zipped herself back into her dress. She straightened the hem of her vintage frock and took one last look at her lipstick before she crossed the room to where I had stood up from my seat.

"Shame on you children keeping secrets." Brit regarded Sonia and me with a grin on her face. "If you kids come to-night I promise a few more prizes for all three of you." She leaned into my shoulder and whispered into my ear, "And you might want to go explain the birds, the bees, and things to the boy wonder. I think he's a bit in a twist."

Sonia jumped off the bed to leave with Brit.

"We are going tonight, right?" Sonia asked.

"Yeah. Give me a call, though. I'll find out if he's up for it." I cocked my head to the side toward the bathroom door to indicate Aaron. The girls kissed me on my cheek as they said their good-byes.

They gathered the last of their things and headed out the door. They giggled their way down the sidewalk as I turned to face Aaron through the bathroom doorway. His thick brows were furrowed into a confused frown above his dark brown eyes; he stared forward without focus, then he looked up at me with questioning eyes.

"You and Sonia both knew?"

"We thought you knew."

"None of you ever said anything and she looks like a girl all the time." He was uncertain of his words and seemed to search for pronouns. "And what she said about Robbie?"

"Well. Brit is usually pretty honest about things. She calls them like she sees 'em and tells the truth." I could tell that Aaron wasn't certain of my explanation.

"Except for one thing?" He scowled back at me.

"Does it really matter? It doesn't change who she is. She's still our friend. Nothing about the person she is has changed. People are allowed to be who they want to be, Aaron. Brit just takes it a bit further." I said everything as defense and not as an explanation. I wanted Aaron to understand it and I wanted him to know we all had the same thing. We all had the safety to be who we wanted to be around one another.

"Do you think other people at the show know?"

"I dunno. But she said she had some more prizes for us tonight if we go."

The confused scowl that Aaron had held since Brit opened the bathroom door was replaced by a playful smile.

"We have to go see what that's about. I want to see the looks on their faces when she comes out as Frank."

I laughed at his excitement and I was relieved that he didn't have any more questions about what Sonia and I had known all along. It was good to see his smile. I reached over and tousled his brown curls into his eyes. Then he surprised me more than he ever had before as he pulled me forward into a hug. He wrapped his arms around my waist and pressed his head to my stomach. I ran my fingers through his headful of curls and I smiled.

We all had the safety to be ourselves with one another.

I had called and told Sonia that it seemed that things were going to be fine with Aaron. We made our plans to go see the show that night. Sonia said she would meet us at the theater. She didn't have a clue what Brit's surprise for us was but she was certain it would be fun no matter what. I had no worries in my mind because Brit had never let us down in the entertainment department.

I coaxed Aaron into the two of us dressing up as Andy and Gerard from the Factory era. We both wore black jeans and striped T-shirts. With Aaron in his biker jacket and me in my black jean jacket we were Warhol-style bookends and we looked essentially the same, but still different.

As we stood in the aisle at the Key Theatre we both scanned the room, looking for Brit or Sonia, until Sonia approached us from the front of the theater. She was wearing the cocktail dress Brit had worn earlier that day and she'd topped it off with a netted pillbox hat that had seen better days.

"Don't you boys look cute?" Sonia moved forward and kissed Aaron on the cheek. It was a quiet gesture to let him know that she was happy he had come through the afternoon and had accepted things as they were.

"Where's the starlet?" I asked as Aaron continued to survey the room.

"She's in back. She said she'd be out to see us before the show starts. We should find some good seats before things fill up." Sonia looked toward the middle section we always sat in and pointed. "There!"

Sonia excused our way into a center row of the theater. We passed a few newbies as well as seasoned creatures of the night and took our seats. Aaron followed right behind Sonia as his eyes continued to search the room for Brit. We all settled into our seats and waited for our starlet to turn up.

Just moments before the houselights blinked on and off Brit made her way up the aisle to our row. She was wrapped tightly in a pink kimono with her hair covered by a scarf. She pushed her way through the knees of everyone seated in the row in front of ours as she graciously made small talk with her admirers along the way. Once she was in front of us she fumbled in her pocket with her back to the screen and took out a small card that was wrapped in a plastic bag.

"Okay, kiddies, let's make this quick. One each—I've gotta get back up front."

She tore small squares of perforated paper from the larger piece of cardstock and handed each one of us a tiny square that was marked with a crudely stamped clover. The three of us sat silently, puzzled by our clovers.

"Um, what is it?" Aaron gazed up at Brit with the question we all shared.

"It's cid, baby. Look, I don't have time to explain, just put it on the tip of your tongue and chew it a bit." Brit nervously retied her kimono. She loosened the sash and tied it again before she looked back at Aaron. "I bring you children a prize and get an interrogation? Just do as Momma tells you and I promise you'll have a divine time with it."

The three of us placed the squares on our tongues and Brit made her way back to the front of the theater. The houselights dimmed as we relaxed into our seats, unsure of what to expect from the clovers. The red lips appeared on the black screen and started their introduction to the show. I could feel myself sink deeper into the velvet of the seat. The first half hour of the film had played before I noticed that everything in the room looked and felt different. The velvet of the seat cushion had turned to liquid beneath my fingertips. I could hear Sonia as she giggled to herself. I turned and looked past Aaron to see what she was laughing at. I could see that Aaron's gaze was fixed on the screen and he had a gigantic smile on his face as his eyes darted about, taking in all the vivid colors of the film. Just past him Sonia stripped down to her bra and half slip, tossed her dress and hat into Aaron's lap, and then stumbled past us and rushed up the aisle. She waved her hands over her head like a game show contestant as she took her place beside Brit at the front of the theater. I stood to follow or stop her and felt Aaron's hand grip my arm as he forced me back into the liquid velvet seat.

"Don't leave me. Stay!" Aaron commanded through clenched teeth.

I melted into the plushness of the velvet as he laced his fingers through mine. My hand tingled, sending electricity through my arm, across my chest, up my neck, into my cheeks. The sensation crawled across my scalp and down my back as pulses of light and energy passed from the palm of Aaron's hand and ran through my entire body as though our energies were fused together. They became an explosion of light as I stared forward at the back of the seat ahead of me. I watched the hair of the person in front of me as it breathed in the dim light from the screen. It waved back and forth like tall grass in a windswept field.

The film itself was just too much to take in. There were too many things going on in it. I tried to focus on the smallest details around me: the electric current that passed between Aaron and me, hair that appeared like fields of grass, the never-ending tunnel of runway lights that marked the center aisle of the theater, and the glowing red exit sign. I had plenty of things to lock my eyes upon to pass my time. The details around me were vivid.

Brit's performance was astounding. At first I didn't recognize her. I'd grown so familiar with her playing the part of the starlet in my life that I wasn't prepared to see her as a man. Not even as the mad scientist in the picture show. But even through the mad hallucinations it all made sense. The role was Brit's through and through. She lived a life beyond the scope of playing Frank. Being in *Rocky Horror* was playing a character for a few hours after midnight in the safe confines of a darkened theater. Being Brit was a lifestyle that defied all conventional notions of gender, a full-time job of suspending reality. She was an amazing star all on her own, but the role and the acid made her radiant.

The show seemed to last longer than usual, as if it played in suspended time. I felt like eleven hours of jaw-clenched hyperreality had passed before the houselights went up. The brightness of the lights caused Aaron to clench my hand. I tried to lift my shoulders from the velvet seat but to no avail—I seemed fused to it. I was stuck in some kind of red velvet taffy. I decided that it was best to let the heat from the bright lights soften the grip the seats had on us before we attempted an escape. The girls walked up the aisle toward us and Sonia looked as though she had been shipwrecked. Her body glistened with sweat, her curls hung damp around her face, and her mascara was streaked from her wild glassy eyes down along her cheeks. Brit was no longer in the costume of Frank but had become an immaculately painted, raven-haired starlet again. She was all the more glamorous as she stood next to the shipwrecked Sonia.

"Aaron, darling. Please don't eat Momma's couture."

I turned to look at Aaron. He had the sleeve of Brit's vintage cocktail frock stuck in the corner of his mouth with his teeth clenched on it. He pulled the dress from his mouth and sheepishly handed it back to Sonia as he gave a timid apology. Sonia took the dress and pulled it over her head. Then she pushed her hair back from her face and smeared the mascara disaster a bit more with her fingertips as she splayed them across her cheeks.

"You boys can't possibly handle breakfast and princess here needs to touch herself up before we face any more unkind lighting." Brit looked all of us over with a smirk as she said a few good-byes to passersby. "Come on, children, let's walk a bit."

Aaron and I stood from our velvet traps. My legs felt like jelly. Aaron caught me as my legs wobbled and his hands gripped my shoulders to hold me upright as the jelly started to become solid again. Brit reached into our row and took my hand to lead me out. I reached back with my other hand and laced my fingers through Aaron's. I felt the electric current as it passed between us. He gave my hand a quick squeeze as he staggered over cardboard cups and popcorn boxes. While I held tightly to Aaron's hand, Brit tucked her hand into the bend of my other elbow and braced me against her weight. Sonia walked a few steps ahead and continued smearing her mascara all over her cheeks as we headed toward the glowing red exit sign.

Once we were outside on the street the air was crisp and fresh. It was full of oxygen and it felt and tasted like the cleanest air I'd ever known, so I inhaled deeply. I heard the noise of the street drawn into me and it filled me with the honking of taxicabs, glowing traffic lights, and music from passing car stereos. It was Georgetown electric with a pulse and beat to it that I'd never felt before. I looked at my friends under the shine of the storefronts and streetlights. They were my superstars and my beautiful friends. Sonia and Aaron both looked around with the same glassy-eyed wonder I had as Brit stood there and touched up her makeup with a powder puff from her compact.

"Oh my god! Oh my god!" Sonia startled us all to attention. "We have to go to the gazebo. We have to! I bet it's beautiful right now."

She turned on her heel and started to walk up Wisconsin Avenue toward R Street while the rest of us looked at one another a moment before we started to walk up the avenue after her. All of us knew the gazebo and were just as desperate as Sonia was to see it that night. She had a half block lead on the rest of us the whole way up the avenue but we all knew our destination when she turned right on R Street. When we turned the corner moments later we could see the back of her dress as she disappeared into the hedges of Dumbarton Oaks.

With the front gates locked at night we had to enter through the hidden service entrance. It was a secret Sonia had discovered on her own before she shared it with the rest of us. Though it was doubtful any of us would recognize the grounds by daylight, the park was our private playground at night. It was a haven of sixteen acres of wilderness hidden in the upper streets of Georgetown with themed terraces, fountains, and pools. The gazebo we all had to see that night was a wisteria-covered terrace just below the rose gardens and above the amphitheater known as the Arbor Terrace. It was our shared sanctuary.

Aaron and I zigzagged a path through the rose gardens down to the fountained terrace staircase as Brit strolled the paths behind us. We knew that Sonia was already at our destination. When I entered the Arbor Terrace with Aaron I could smell the scent of roses and raw dirt heavy in the air. I could see Sonia in the shadows, then the flick of her lighter illuminated her face with an orange glow as she inhaled to light a cigarette. She stood with her feet bare in the pool that sat between two benches. As she took her first puff off her cigarette she studied a stone face that was hung on the wall.

"He thought he knew it all. But look at how he fucked up all of the kids. Hera was wise to him and she got fed up with his shit." Pointing at the face of Zeus or whatever other god it might have been in front of her, she filled the space with pluming cigarette smoke, then turned to watch as Brit made her entrance into the arbor.

"Oh, darlin'. Hera was a bitch, too. She hated those kids. She was jealous of all the gifts Daddy gave 'em." Our starlet entered the arbor and sat on a bench. "She still had nothin' on Brit's mommy though." She rummaged through her pocket-book for an elastic band. Once it was found she used the loop of black elastic cord to sweep her hair away from her face and into a high ponytail. Then she crossed her legs and straightened her hem before leaning forward and resting her elbows on her knees. "Momma's gonna tell you kiddies how Miss Brit came to be. Okay?"

Sonia stepped out of the fountain and took a seat on the ledge behind the bench Aaron and I shared. I reached up and took the cigarette from her hand so I could take a drag, then I offered it back to her. She waved the return off and her eyes focused on Brit as she eagerly awaited the starlet's story.

"Can I get one of those?" Aaron timidly asked.

Sonia handed him her pack of cigarettes and her lighter. Aaron lit a cigarette, reclined on the bench, and rested his head in my lap as he looked up into the wisteria-twined arches above us.

Brit began her story, and we all listened intently to it. She told us a story of a sad little boy from Rockville. He was named Brian Hammond. The boy was the only son of a German man and a Chinese woman who shared a life in the suburbs. Brian was different from the other suburban teens—he was more sensitive and preferred the company of girls. The kids at school teased him. Not only was he effeminate but his almond-shaped eyes and dark hair had him labeled a *chink*.

His father traveled extensively as a civilian engineer for the military and his mother made the home a strict and cold Chinese household in the father's absence. Brian was unhappy with his life until one day in 1983 when a man came and installed cable television in the den of the Rockville home. After that happened he would rush home every day after school and watch music videos on MTV until his mother called him to dinner. It was from these videos that he learned the beauty of the New Wave music being exported from England. He watched Duran Duran, Adam Ant, and the other New Romantics. He grew enamored of the gender-bending acts of Eurythmics, Boy George, Pete Burns, and, finally, Marilyn.

Marilyn was a boy pop star and a friend of Boy George. Though he was a boy, Marilyn was the spitting image of the screen goddess Marilyn Monroe. The pop star made a strong impression on Brian.

What followed Brian's MTV education were acts that could be regarded as nothing short of alchemy. He started to work at his own reinvention by making himself in the image of the two Marilyns. At first, Brian kept his transformation a secret. He locked his bedroom door and dressed up in front of his mirror late at night. He studied magazines and taught himself to copy makeup and hair styles from the glossy pictures. All through the night he perfected himself. He learned how to place cosmetics so that they would soften his features and make him appear more feminine. Along with the makeup he practiced and retrained his voice to affect the breathy manner of Marilyn Monroe.

Early one afternoon Brian had started his transformation without his customary certainty that his mother was asleep for her daily nap, and he had forgotten to lock his door. He was dressed in a thrift-store party dress with hot rollers in his hair. Just as he'd started working the pancake makeup into his face the door opened. His mother stood in the doorway and held his freshly folded laundry. They both froze for a moment and stared, stunned by each other. Brian's mother dropped the laundry on the floor and stormed through the house in a rage. She screamed in broken English about perverts, shame, disgust, anger, and heartbreak, and she blamed Brian's father for never being around. Brian quickly wiped the foundation from his face with a bath towel and ran to the kitchen to try and calm his mother, but nothing worked. Still enraged, she picked up a paring knife from the countertop and lunged toward him.

Brian felt a sharp shocking pain in his chest. He looked down and saw the paring knife suspended three fingers above his left nipple. He'd been stabbed by his own mother.

Brian looked at the knife that was buried an inch into his chest before he raised his eyes to his mother. He saw that her eyes were wild and her breath was heavy. He thought she looked like an animal. With a quick jerk of his right hand, he pulled the knife from his chest and felt a wet, burning pain as the blade came out. He looked his mother in the eye as he set the knife back on the counter.

"You fucking bitch."

Brian glared at the woman who had stabbed him.

His mother began to scream. She no longer screamed at him but instead at herself. She slapped her own face and collapsed onto the kitchen floor as she wailed. Brian ran to a neighbor's house and started to pound furiously on the door. His neighbor opened the door with a shocked look on her face as she tried to understand the sight of a young boy in a party dress with blood oozing from his chest.

"My mother stabbed me. Help." Brian fainted on his neighbor's doorstep.

The neighbor called an ambulance and the police. Brian was taken to the emergency room, where the superficial knife wound was stitched up. Over the years the wound faded to a scar that Brian would conceal under a padded bra. It was only those closest to him who would ever see the mark left there or hear any story about how he'd gained it. The police came and interviewed Brian at the hospital. A caseworker from social services talked to him as well. All of them told Brian they would protect him.

He and his father saw each other for the last time at a custody hearing. His mother refused to attend the hearing and his father said little and just stared at Brian the entire time the lawyer and the social worker argued their positions to the judge. It was as though Brian's father was trying to recognize the son he wanted beneath the girl Brian was becoming. He signed Brian over to social services at that hearing. Brian never heard from his mother or his father again.

Though he was never threatened in foster care, no one understood how to help a boy like Brian. Each new family he tried to live with sent him to psychiatrists and therapists while they encouraged him to be a boy again. But Brian didn't want that. He knew that he was special. No one in any of his new homes thought his specialness would come to anything good. They all tried to change him, so he ran away.

The last time Brian ran away, he rode the Metrorail into the city and never returned to foster care. Instead he discovered Georgetown, with its beautiful homes, decadent storefronts, and busy avenues. He fell in love with the streets of Georgetown while he slept in garages, gardens, and under bridges. During the day he hung out in the punk shops like Smash and Commander Salamander as he daydreamed of a life that resembled the glossy pictures he found in fashion magazines discarded in the trash bins behind the news shops. All while he panhandled for spare change and leftovers from the fine bistros that lined the avenues. He saved his spare change to dress himself in vintage frocks from the thrift store he'd found down on K Street. He freshened himself up and did his makeup in the public bathrooms of the Georgetown Park mall while he stashed his things in the parking garage below. No one who passed him on the streets mistook him for being a boy or would have ever guessed that his wardrobe was hidden in a waste bin. In a city built on appearances, he just seemed to be a glamorous young girl looking for a bit of change to make a phone call or buy a Metro ticket.

One night Brian walked down Wisconsin Avenue later than usual, heading toward the parking garage at Georgetown Park to find a spot to sleep for the night. When he turned the bend at Prospect Street, for the first time he saw the beautiful androgynous creatures teeming in front of the Key Theatre. Brian had just enough cash from the day's panhandling to buy one ticket to the *The Rocky Horror Picture Show*.

Brian sat and watched the movie with tears in his eyes.

He had a sense that he had finally found people who could understand a boy like him. He couldn't take his eyes off either the lead on the screen or the boy who acted out the role at the front of the theater. At the end of the film, Brian summoned all his courage, walked down the aisle, and introduced himself to the most beautiful man he'd ever seen.

Robbie was intrigued by Brian and invited him to join the cast for breakfast after the show. They walked the two blocks from the theater to Au Pied de Cochon and were escorted to the grand banquette in the back room. Brian felt as though he had landed in a big Hollywood movie. A beautiful man treating him to breakfast and making him the center of attention. He felt like Marilyn Monroe in *Gentlemen Prefer Blondes*.

After breakfast the two of them took a cab up Wisconsin Avenue to Robbie's apartment, which was across the street from the Russian embassy. Brian never slept in garages after that night. With Robbie he found a home.

Robbie worked in an exclusive salon on M Street when he was not being Frank, and after business hours, Robbie helped Brian complete his transformation from the suburban schoolboy into the beautiful girl he'd always dreamed of being. With his hair, makeup, waxing, and manicures done in the same salon as the wives of politicians and diplomats, Brian felt like a real girl when he was with Robbie. The metamorphosis was so real that he started to work in the salon as a receptionist, with no notice of the boy he had been back in Rockville. He was a beautiful blonde with the looks of a vintage Hollywood starlet. Inspired by Brian's love of Vivienne Westwood, Malcolm McLaren, the Sex Pistols, Boy George, and the UK fashion magazines, Robbie picked a new name for the girl Brian had become. Brian became Brit.

"So you see, Andy . . . a less than average boy can make himself into anything he wants to be."

Brit had ended her story with that personal message to me. She had seen herself in me from our first meeting. Our friendship was one of empathy, knowing, understanding, acceptance, and respect. We both understood that self-actualization is possible even though it can be a hard thing to commit to. Andy had done it. He had turned the everyday into art while he reinvented himself and created the Factory, where others could do the same.

I looked at my friends that night as Brit stood to leave the arbor. I wondered what was ahead for us. I hoped and dreamed that we could find a way to become ourselves and live our lives with truth and art.

Sonia stood and wiped tears from her eyes as she crossed the arbor and hugged Brit. I looked down at Aaron's head in my lap and saw that the faintest tears had streaked from his eyes to the edges of his temples. He had curled his arm into the small of my back with his thumb hooked through my belt loop to embrace me. I shivered and my teeth started to chatter. Aaron sat up, took off his jacket, and draped it over my shoulders while he hugged me to his chest. He rubbed both my arms up and down through the jacket with his palms as he held me close to warm me.

"Those were good drugs," Aaron deadpanned.

The sky shifted to a dark gray. Brit walked home with Sonia, and Aaron and I walked back to my apartment. We were unable to sleep. We buzzed with our shared electricity as we sat on my bed and conceived our next film.

Those drugs were good, indeed.

The next film was *Drugs*.

Sonia did not appear in the film. Instead, she stood by my side as a silent assistant director.

Aaron and Brit had gathered their supplies for the film over a few days. The project was Aaron's experiment with a stockpile of drugs. Our introduction to escapism with LSD had left Aaron fascinated by the transcendental properties of narcotics. Committing their use to film had become his obsession and he had everything planned, with Brit's assistance. Sonia and I were just there to run the camera and perhaps to keep things from getting ugly. We were the sober eyes to watch over the stars in case the paramedics needed to be called.

The concept was to make an instructional film for recreational drug use. I'd returned to filming with cartridges and the Bell + Howell camera. The hard spotlights were aimed at my bed as Aaron and Brit returned as my superstars with their assorted paraphernalia spread across the sheets and arranged on the nightstand.

I set the camera up on the tripod and took a few Polaroids to check the light. I looked at the framing caught on the instant film, then I handed the images to Sonia. She crossed the room to crumple the sheets on the bed. I took a couple more Polaroids to see her adjustments and I passed them to Aaron for his approval. Brit touched up her makeup with a sponge from her compact as I checked the framing of the scene through the viewfinder of the movie camera.

"Are you two ready to start?"

Sonia crossed to the bed and fluffed the pillows again as Aaron pulled his T-shirt up over his head and tossed it at me with a laugh.

"Lights and action, Andy!"

Aaron had never called me Andy before that and the room was silenced by it. There was a tension in the air. The girls exchanged glances with me while they waited for some cue to base their next moves upon. I looked at Aaron for a moment. He was shirtless. His golden skin and lean athletic torso displayed against the white pillows with the frayed waistband of his jeans resting at his hips. I studied the details. I saw the physical parts that were an aesthetic fascination for me. I scanned up to his face, his lips in a playful smirk. There was no malice when he called me Andy. He was being playful and exuberant.

I took another look through the viewfinder and framed the shot to be certain that Aaron was the central figure.

"Art is what you can get away with. Action."

I pressed the trigger and stepped back from the camera ,where I stood shoulder to shoulder with Sonia. We waited and watched.

The first reel of film was of smoke. Aaron couldn't figure out how to roll a joint so Brit snatched the papers and the pot away from him and wrapped one up like a pro without smudging her lipstick at all. Sonia fanned the smoke away from her face as she scurried around the apartment, lighting incense and stuffing towels around the door frames. I stood behind the camera and watched Aaron and Brit laugh at nothingness. The smoke had gently dumbed them down. I didn't like the smell of it and its effect on the two of them left me with no interest in it for myself. I was worried that it might not even make a good film because nothing interesting happened. They were just stoned. There was no action.

I let the cartridge run to the end and loaded a new one. I waited to pull the camera's trigger until the next part of the experiment was started. Each cartridge could capture just over three minutes of action. Watching Brit and Aaron stoned lacked any action whatsoever—I didn't think it was worth more film. When the stupor of the stars eased, the next scene opened. I pressed the trigger and remained behind the camera.

With my typical short film titles the second reel could have been called *Blow* or *Snow*. I'd never witnessed anyone on cocaine before that day. As I stood behind the camera, I watched it unfold as something new to my eyes. Brit had set a hand mirror on the center of the bed and used a razor blade to chop the white powder as she spread it back and forth across the surface, eventually settling on a series of lines spread into short rails. Brit pulled her hair back into a ponytail that she secured with an elastic band from around her wrist. She rolled a dollar bill into a tube, then she leaned over the mirror and inhaled two of the rails quickly up her nostrils. She dabbed her index finger in the residue on the mirror and rubbed her finger across her gums as she passed the dollar tube to Aaron. He tucked his wavy hair behind his ears, then he leaned forward over the mirror and did exactly as he had seen Brit do. As he rose from the mirror a smile broadened across his face.

The effect of cocaine made a good film. I loaded another cartridge into the camera. The superstars had become confident and animated as Sonia and I stood and watched them. They chattered as they kept no train of thought constant. Brit obsessively tidied things on the nightstand and paced in front of the bed. Aaron seemed to be grinding his teeth between his wild bursts of ideas for more films we could make. Brit assured him that they were all fantastic ideas. They laughed with each other and talked to us even though we were outside of the frame. Unlike their performance on the smoke reel, they were happy and alive. It was good film. Aaron smiled broadly as his eyes beamed euphorically. Every now and then we locked eyes and I would smile at him, then he would gently bite his lip as he raised a brow and laughed at the recognition he'd gotten from me. This playful flirtation repeated like that until the mirror had been cleared of the cocaine.

I loaded another cartridge of film into the camera and waited. The last part of the film changed everything between the four of us. It was the brick that shattered the window into our world together. The last substance in the experiment was heroin. Brit paused to ask Aaron if he was sure he wanted to go on. Without a thought he nodded his head and smirked.

"Yeah."

Brit suggested they each snort a bit first before they moved on to the other way and Aaron agreed. The effect of heroin seemed to be the opposite of the cocaine, though it was done in the same way. As I watched them I felt a sickness in my stomach. They were in a place that was unknown to me. What we witnessed made Sonia and me restless.

"Are they okay?" Sonia whispered.

"Dunno. They're breathing."

"It's fine," Brit replied, her words drawn long and deep, then she reached over and slapped Aaron gently on the cheek a few times to rouse him from his trance.

"That's wild. It felt like we were on television there for a minute." Aaron shook his head to get his bearings on the room again. He had a confused grin on his face.

"Television?"

I didn't understand what he meant by that.

"Yeah. That didn't make any sense, did it?" He nodded and laughed to himself.

Sonia folded her arms across her chest. She was silent but I could tell she had lost her patience with the project. Her face had turned stone cold and her breathing was heavier. Her nostrils flared as she glared at the other superstars.

Brit pulled a few things from her handbag. They were a length of rubber tubing, a lighter, and two plastic packages. She then crossed the apartment out of the camera's frame to get a glass of water from the bathroom sink. I looked through the viewfinder and saw Aaron as he remained on the bed with the gear. He picked up one of the packages and tore away the plastic to expose a syringe. When he did, Sonia looked at me as her crossed arms turned into a tense grip. Brit prepared the next part of the experiment. She appeared to be like a chef or a scientist as she mixed water with the drug and used the lighter to melt it all together. Aaron watched carefully as Brit filled the syringes with her mixture.

"If I show you, can you stick yourself?" Brit asked.

"Um, what happens if I miss?" Aaron's voice quivered in betrayal of his confidence and curiosity.

"You don't want to miss. I'll do it for you this time. But you're going to have to learn to do it yourself after."

Aaron nodded and Brit moved forward on the bed with a syringe grasped in her teeth as she wrapped the tubing around Aaron's biceps. She tapped at the inside bend of his elbow until the vein swelled. She took the syringe from her mouth and removed the cap, then she pressed the syringe until a drop of the liquid came out of the tip. She moved in closer to see the spot where the vein bulged from Aaron's arm. Her eyes glanced up at his face. It was a questioning glance to which Aaron nodded his reply. Brit looked back down at the fattened vein and stabbed into it with the needle. Aaron's face winced at the poke and he looked away as Brit pulled the shaft of the syringe back and mixed Aaron's blood with the liquid inside before she pushed the plunger down and loosened the tubing from around his arm. Aaron's jaw relaxed and his body sagged limp against the headboard with the pillows crumpled beneath his weight. Brit quickly repeated the whole procedure on herself, then drifted into a similar recline right next to Aaron. The room was silent. Sonia and I stood shoulder to shoulder as we watched them. I glanced to my left and could see Sonia as she wiped her eyes. There were tears on her cheeks and she wiped them away again but she couldn't stop them as fast as they came. Finally, she broke the silence.

"This is bullshit. I can't watch them like this."

With those words Sonia pushed past me and my camera as she left the apartment. I stood in silence and watched the two superstars as they drifted somewhere that was unknown to me. Was it like they were on television? What did Aaron mean? I heard the cartridge in the camera click to its end and loaded another one to continue the film.

With the last cartridge I broke from my rule of leaving the camera steady and making no adjustments. I turned the lens to get a tight close-up on Aaron's face. He was glassy-eyed and numb with his mouth slightly opened. His eyes gazed forward as he seemed to watch something that I couldn't see. A faint bit of foamed saliva crept from the corners of his cracked lips. He seemed like a zombie at first glance but I knew he'd found something he lacked otherwise. He'd found a kind of peace or a release. As though the mildest of tension had been erased.

Aaron had found an escape. Through art I had reconciled our feelings for each other. It was a safe place for me to keep things. Our relationship was aesthetic for me, subject and voyeur.

But, there was less for Aaron in that arrangement. Adoration is not touch. Drugs provided him with euphoria and perhaps they released him from any self-conscious feelings he felt from my gaze. It made sense to me, but I didn't know how we could ever be anything else. Hallucinations, euphoria, or whatever the high brought him let Aaron escape the stress and denial of what we had.

With that realization I pressed the trigger to stop the film. I sat at my desk and watched them. I waited for them to come back to reality. Brit was the first to rouse from the trance of the drug. When she did, she looked around the room and then seemed to get her bearings with a deep inhalation of air. Once she pulled out of the fog she checked on Aaron. He was still deep in the trance they had shared. She looked over at me and assured me that he would come out of it. She pulled the waste bin from under my desk and placed it next to the bed at Aaron's side. She told me he might need to use it when he came out of the high. Then she packed her things back into her handbag and left the apartment.

I was alone in my apartment with Aaron adrift. The heroin scene was the last cut of film I ever made. I sat on the bed next to him and watched his chest move as he breathed shallow breaths. He had a vacant expression on his face and the room was silent around us. I lay next to him and tried to make my breath shallow and paced with his. I couldn't force myself to breathe that way. I sat and watched his profile for any changes. It was a few moments before his eyes brightened with the recognition of place. He knew he was in my apartment as he took a deep breath of air and lunged forward with a spew of vomit. I fumbled around the side of the bed and tried to hand him the trash can but the effort was wasted and he got sick all over my disheveled sheets.

I watched him as he fought his way back to life and out of the trance. His body shook as if the room were freezing. He grabbed my hand and it seemed that he expected me to pull him the rest of the way out. I held his hand and sat with him. I pulled him close to my chest in a hug. It was an embrace to assure him that I was there for him. His sweat soaked from his brow into my shirt. I pushed his hair back from his face. He was damp with sweat and his body trembled as he buried his face into my chest and took deep breaths. He coughed against the depth of the air that filled his lungs.

"Can I stay with you tonight, please?" he mumbled into my shirt.

"Yeah, but let's get you and my bed cleaned up."

"I'm sorry. I didn't know I was gonna puke." Tears filled his eyes as he looked at the mess of sheets and bile.

"It's okay. We'll put them in the wash and get you into the shower."

"Will you help me?"

"Yeah, Aaron. No problem."

I left him on the bed as I walked into the bathroom and turned on the shower, tossing a dry towel over the curtain rod.

"I mean, shower with me." He scrunched his face into a question. It was as though he expected rejection from me.

I looked at him for a moment. He was beautifully fragile. He was my best and truest friend. My first love. I offered my hand to him and he took hold of it and laced his fingers through mine, then I led him into the bathroom, where I undressed him and placed him under the streams of hot water. I undressed myself and stepped into the shower with him. With his head bowed to his chest I ran the bar of green striped soap across his chest, down both of his legs, and along his back. I turned him around under the streams of water to rinse the suds from him. He glanced at the green soap in the dish before he looked into my eyes.

"Hey, we use the same soap."

His eyes brightened into a smile and he pulled me into a hug. We stood under the water in that hug until the water started to run cold. Afterward, I wrapped him in blankets and changed the sheets on the bed. I didn't sleep that night. I lay there in my bed and held him close as his body shuddered. The whole night his legs twitched and he shivered, even though his skin burned up with heat and night sweats. I was thrilled to hold him close to me but I was fearful of what his body went through from the drugs.

Aaron's first film idea was the start of his descent into addiction. I took my time sending the reels away in the mailers. I didn't want to see what the finished film looked like. I never spliced it together and never screened *Drugs* for anyone, not even Aaron.

It was the last film I made with any of my superstars.

Brit and Aaron drifted into other worlds and lost interest in making films. For Brit drugs were but another form of entertainment; she could take them or leave them. But for Aaron, it was as though he'd found a way to avoid sorting out his sense of self and our relationship. If he stayed high enough he didn't have to answer the questions none of us were prepared to confront. In the induced euphoria there was no desire, no love, and every expression of such things that slipped through could be blamed on a blackout or attributed to the drugs themselves.

Sonia had no interest in that kind of diversion. Though she had often dismissed Peter as being too dull, the drugs caused her to seek him out again. Our art-making had taken a dark turn and Peter was her escape from that.

I spent more time alone in the galleries, where I found my sanctuary from our changes that troubled me. The paintings didn't change. I could renew my vision of them, but they didn't fundamentally change.

The four of us had shared so much as we moved from childhood to something else. But we couldn't stay that way forever. It was springtime in Washington and the cherry blossoms around the monuments had started to pop. I walked around the tidal basin under the pink clouds of the blossoms. Alone.

We drifted apart.

love (illness)

A new school year started without Aaron. It was my senior year of high school. I should have been making plans and preparing myself for college. Instead it was a rough start. I was consumed with worries and couldn't think of anything I wanted to do with my life.

I couldn't seem to think about anything but where Aaron was and how he was doing. Last I knew, he'd been put in Sibley Memorial Hospital. I hadn't seen him throughout most of the summer. Sibley was where Dr. Moore sent his more troubled patients, and drugs had made Aaron one of those. Aaron's father had quickly signed him over to the doctor and the hospital so that his troubles could be handled on a secured floor. There was no contact between us, but the school rumor squad made certain I knew where he was.

I feared that he had already been damaged beyond repair. His time in the hospital was lonelier for me than the time before he came to the day school. I couldn't bear the sadness and anger. At the same time I wished for his safety, I wished I had never met him. If I had never known him or talked to him, I would have been ignorant of how much I could miss him. Being *without* is tolerable when you don't know anything else. Only once you've known *with,* without is torture.

I was so confused by my experience of what had happened that I couldn't find the words to ask Dr. Moore about Aaron's condition. The time we spent in his office without Aaron felt as though the doctor was just waiting me out, waiting for me to confess how I felt.

I missed Aaron. But I couldn't figure out what we were to each other so I made a list of all the things we were not.

We were not brothers, cousins, or any kind of family.

He was not my boyfriend.

We were not lovers.

He wasn't my pet.

He wasn't my child.

Yet the pain I felt throughout my body made me think he could have been any of those things or all of them. And I was again feeling the things that the sight of him had erased.

I wanted to vanish or become invisible.

I wanted to die.

"Aaron misses you. He asks about you every day. He's

worried about you. Worried that you might be angry with him and worried that you're sad. He worries more for you than himself. Are you angry with him, Caleb?"

We returned to our regular appointments once the school year started, but it had taken the doctor three weeks to break through my silence and pain. He had tried to let me bring it up first, but it became clear that I wouldn't. I'd been quiet all summer plus these three weeks, but Aaron asked about me every day.

"I'm not angry with him. Is he going to get better?"

Dr. Moore looked at me for a few moments as his strategy ran through his head. He had helped grow the intimacy Aaron and I shared in his office over the years. Yet we wouldn't display it any further than a staged kiss for him. We had found our own way to love each other through the art we created as artist, muse, subject, and voyeur. I didn't know what Aaron might have called it, I just knew that we had something very different from what was normal.

"Caleb, how do you feel about Aaron?"

"I'm worried about him. I want him to get well."

I didn't want to sort through my feelings. I was afraid that the relationship we had and our inability to act upon it was the real source of Aaron's problems. The doctor had facilitated our experimentation and encouraged our artistic collaborations but I didn't want to share Aaron with the doctor anymore. My fears about the role I might have played in Aaron's problems kept me mute. In my mind I struggled with my own questions about everything. I knew we loved each other. I knew that the encouragement the doctor gave us to act upon that feeling was wrong, since he seemed to enjoy it as a form of entertainment. The doctor was a voyeur himself, and we were his subjects. Our actions and desires had been guarded secrets, and secrets always feel wrong.

The love didn't feel wrong to me, but Aaron clearly struggled with it. My mind posed questions and I wasn't certain that I wanted to accept the obvious answers to them. I was afraid that whatever I found would betray us somehow. I was afraid that someone would use my feelings to hurt Aaron. I didn't know who or how, it was just a sense that I would be responsible for more pain for him.

I remembered our last week at the day school when he had defended me. I thought of the things that James had said and Aaron's insistence that it wasn't true. He had tried to prove his point with his fists and rage. I'd seen the tears he fought as he walked away from James, and his lasting anger at the single word that had been used as an insult. He had fought for me and had been sent away early for it. I thought of his fight and I didn't want to betray him with my words. It seemed to me that he didn't want it to be true, for either of us.

Faggot.

"Is he going to be okay?" I said nothing more than that.

It was a question asked in a flat tone. I felt my stomach and heart tremble but I asked it in a monotone and controlled manner. It was my Andy voice, the practiced and robotic tone I used whenever I wanted to hide my true emotions.

The doctor stood up and walked around to the front of his desk. He sat on the edge of the desk directly in front of me, crossed his arms, and never took his eyes off me. He examined me with his gaze and he tried to detect any sign of emotions hidden beneath the flat tone of my voice before he proceeded with our discussion.

"He has a great deal of work to do to be okay, Caleb. You should know that there are times when addiction is a symptom and not the cause of a patient's problem. Aaron's cause is his feelings. He doesn't know what to do with his feelings and heroin helps him put them under his control. He'll be okay. But he's going to need your help to do so. Caleb, do you understand what I'm saying?"

I nodded yes and our session ended with my answer. The doctor circled back to his seat and started writing in his journal.

"Would you like me to tell Aaron anything for you, Caleb?"

I didn't have anything to say. I didn't want to say something that would cause Aaron to have more trouble. I didn't want the doctor to be a part of what we had.

"Tell him I want him to get well and come back to school."

I left the office and walked to the Hirshhorn. I sat on the bench in front of the lips. It was the bench I sat on every time I needed to clear my head and think. It was where I came for sanctuary and meditation with Andy. As I sat there I thought about what the doctor had said about Aaron and the feelings that caused him to become an addict. I understood because I felt them, too. It was love, but it was love that would make us different.

I looked at the lips and wondered.

How could I help Aaron if I was the cause of his problem and the feelings he had?

Sonia started back to school with her own set of problems. Over the summer her parents had separated. Her mother just flatly couldn't stand being married for another moment and she and Sonia had moved into an apartment building nestled along Rock Creek. The building was like the others near the Kalorama Triangle, with European grandeur, high ceilings, and a one-word name: the Ontario.

The divorce was a bitter one, as most Washington social divorces were. Status and assets were at stake. Sonia wasn't fazed by any of that. She had never had any delusions about her parents having affection for each other. She knew that their marriage had been all for show.

The divorce had its advantages for Sonia. Even though she had moved with her mother, she was free to come and go as she pleased between the Ontario and the Georgetown house. Her behavior was unseen and unchecked as her parents exchanged barbs through lawyers. The divorce helped Sonia become a grown woman while she was still in high school.

Whenever her father was away for medical conferences, she and I had the Georgetown home to ourselves. We played house there. Sonia also had use of her father's most beloved possession, his navy-blue Porsche 928.

"We're taking a field trip!" Sonia shook the key chain to the Porsche in my face while we sat in her kitchen and binged on croissants from the American Cafe.

"Um, where?" I pulled at the horn of a croissant and watched the flaky pastry unravel in the air between us.

"Just because we play hooky twice a week doesn't mean everyone in town does. Don't worry about it. It's an adventure and it'll cheer you up. And are you going to wear those damn things all day?" Sonia gestured at my white Vuarnet sunglasses.

Sonia hated the Vuarnets. They had been a gift from Aaron. He had bought the Vuarnets on a ski trip the previous winter and I fell in love with them instantly. They were my most treasured possession. It could have been anything and they would have been precious to me. They were big with white plastic frames and had ridiculously dark lenses. They weren't like the Ray-Bans everyone else was wearing and were so unchic that I thought they were cool. Aaron had been so proud of them when he gave them to me. His excitement about them felt like love.

Sonia led me to the carriage house, we climbed into the prized sports car, and she pushed the remote control to open the garage door. When she turned the key in the ignition the car growled to a start. Carefully she backed out and stopped the car once she had it lined up to exit the alleyway.

"Listen."

She pressed the gas pedal to the floor and the tires squealed as we shot up the alleyway. We zigzagged our way through the Georgetown streets to Clara Barton Parkway and into Maryland. After a half-hour drive around the Beltway we arrived at the Sandy Spring Friends School. Sonia parked the Porsche in the faculty parking lot.

"They won't dare tow it. They'll be afraid to. It might belong to a building fund donor." She laughed at the privilege afforded to the owners of luxury cars.

We made our way to the cafeteria and found Peter sitting at a table with his friends.

"Come sit with us somewhere. I brought someone for you to meet," Sonia instructed Peter as we stood at the side of the table.

I could see a faint resemblance to Aaron in Peter. It wasn't as great a resemblance as Sonia had always said but there was something there. He wore his hair buzzed short, while Aaron would never sacrifice his beautiful mane of curls. Peter was a bit paler and thinner than Aaron, too. There were enough similarities to remind me painfully of Aaron, but it wasn't a match.

We sat at an empty table with Sonia and me on one side and Peter across from us.

"So, you're Caleb?"

"Yeah."

"Sonia talks about you a lot. You're like a brother to her." He reached forward, pausing with his hand near the frames of the Vuarnets. "May I?"

I sat still as he pulled the glasses away from my eyes. His caramel-brown eyes stared into mine and he smiled.

"Same ice storm as Sonia. You two are trouble. You're gonna get me into trouble."

"No trouble here, Pete," Sonia replied from beside me.

Peter handed the glasses back to me and continued to smile. He never broke his eye contact with me even as Sonia talked to him.

"Come on. Just ditch and let's go to the aquarium or something."

"I can't just ditch like you guys at the institute do. They actually pay attention to us here."

"Peter, they're Quakers. It's not like they're gonna discipline you."

"Nah, I can't. We'll do something over winter break. I promise."

"You're beginning to get dull." Sonia waved her hand at him in a dismissive manner. "Come on, Caleb. Let's go play."

We stood from the table and Peter remained seated.

"It was good to meet you, Caleb. I hope to see you again sometime."

"Thanks. Um, me too."

Aaron sprung himself out of rehab with a secret. It was our secret with his embellishment. He had a breakthrough one day in group therapy. He revealed that he had a truth to tell. It was a truth that opened the doors of the secured floor and allowed him to walk out and never sit in a therapist's office again.

Aaron told a roomful of patients and doctors that Dr. Elliot Moore had used the two of us for his own voyeuristic entertainment. The confession chronicled our relationship over the years as some kind of sexual abuse. Dr. Moore had never touched either one of us himself, but in Aaron's account of things it seemed that the doctor had guided us to molest each other.

That wasn't the way I had seen things. That wasn't the way I remembered. I had convinced myself that the doctor had helped us, protected us, and given us a safe place to express our feelings. It was shelter that had been provided. I knew that Aaron and I were different from other people. I knew that difference didn't fit into the world we lived in. We couldn't talk about what we had together without shame and fear. The doctor had seen it from the start and given us a safe haven to express ourselves. He'd given us a place where we could love each other in a protected environment away from disapproving eyes. Within the shelter of the doctor's office we explored our sexuality out of sight of the ignorant and judgmental.

I didn't know what to make of Aaron's account of all that had happened in the doctor's office. I had always protected our secrets; they were moments I held precious. Sure, at times I thought the doctor was crossing a line. I suspected he might be aroused by the situations he staged and encouraged. I didn't feel it was abuse though, just another form of voyeurism. It had provided us the opportunity to touch, to kiss, and to create art. It couldn't have all been wrong. I feared that Aaron's confession nullified his feelings for me. I was confused and felt betrayed.

The confession earned Aaron his freedom. He had bartered our secrets in order to escape the place that could repair him. Upon his release a storm of fury, anger, and blame started.

Our fathers worked quickly to have Elliot Moore's access to any hospital or treatment facility suspended. Gossip of our alleged abuse circulated through town in hushed tones. The doctor lost his license and was branded a pedophile. It took less than two weeks for them to put him out of business and run him out of town. Elliot Moore received the blame for every problem we were thought to have had. He was held accountable for everything different, peculiar, or troubled about us. Within a month of the revelations, a real estate agent had a sign in front of the brownstone, and the doctor was rumored to have disappeared forever. He would never provide boys like us a place for exploration again.

Aaron came out of the hospital changed. Maybe he had already changed over the summer when I hadn't seen him, but once he was back at school for me to see, the changes became very clear. He stopped playing soccer and skipped classes constantly. He wasn't a boy anymore and he didn't want to be mistaken for naive or gentle ever again. It wasn't as though he had become mean, but he had become tough. He didn't care about anything anymore.

Everyone at school had heard of our problems with Dr. Moore. The story was just the type of sensational gossip that students of the institute thrived on. It became Aaron's free pass to do as he pleased and suffer no repercussions for it.

The only person who didn't play along with the pardon was Sonia. When Aaron came back to school he stepped out of line with her. She was willing to be there for him and he laughed it off. He mocked her for being friends with all of us and called her a name I never imagined he could call her.

Fag hag.

The wall went up between them after that.

"The boy wonder came out an asshole."

"He's having a hard time. He'll be okay."

"No. No way. People have a hard time every day. He's an asshole. I'm not in the mood to have him take me down and you shouldn't be either."

"Come on, Sonia. You're not being fair."

"Fair? I never did shit to him and he's being an asshole. He stalks around here acting like no one can touch him because he's had it so rough. Seems to me like you two had plenty of fun together without the doctor. Sure that guy was out of line but I don't think any of this is about being fair. You two went through it together and you're not an asshole. Are you going to become one, too? Just to be fair?"

"No. It's just . . . you know how sensitive he is. He's made this stuff with Elliot a big deal. Yeah, the stuff that happened was wrong, but he's just having a hard time."

"Nope. Bullshit. Asshole."

I didn't have a response. Sonia wasn't interested in one anyway. Aaron had fucked up with her and once she shut down she also shut people out. The only thing to be gained if I had tried to explain things further would've been getting shut out myself. I only had one reply and it didn't make her happy. It just stopped the conversation.

"I'm sorry. I'll try to talk to him."

There was no talking to Aaron. Instead, I had to remain patient while I listened to him as he ranted and planned. Throughout all of it I hoped that one day he would get the rage out of his system. I wanted him to be like he had been before when he was tender and gentle. I tried to remember what his smile looked like as I watched his eyes and waited for something I knew to come back to them. I remained silent but nothing changed or softened. His eyes were always nervous and filled with an expression that didn't suit him. His eyes had gone wild. Yet, I refused to give up on him. He was my best friend. With no certainty of anything else, I knew I couldn't let go of the one thing I'd known. So, I waited patiently and he led us. My carefully drawn world of superstars had fallen apart and I had nothing beautiful left to hold on to but my memories. I was no longer the director of our films or art projects. Without the art, everything descended into chaos.

Aaron's anger was fed more as his father tried to take control of the aftermath of the scandal and get family life back on track. Annoyed by the meddling, Aaron decided that we should run. It was two weeks before my sixteenth birthday. We didn't go far but we did run away from the comfort and shelter of our parents' homes.

I celebrated my birthday away from my family with Aaron. No one had bothered to acknowledge my birthday ever since I had turned thirteen. I didn't fit the picture-perfect life my stepmother wanted so I was ignored. On the run with Aaron and without rules it was finally a birthday party. For one day Aaron eased up the wild ride and showered me with his affection. He took me to the Hirshhorn, where we wandered the galleries in silence and ate birthday cake while we sat on the curb outside. Though we had no real plans outside of our daydreams, my birthday made me feel like there was some hope for us. The hope didn't last long past that day.

Our first stop was Brit and Robbie's. The four of us shared a studio apartment like it was some kind of extended sleepover. Aaron and I stopped going to school and explored the city while our hosts were at work. At night, we snuck into the bars of Dupont Circle with our fake IDs from the Electromax on M Street. For many of them ID wasn't even required. The proprietors looked the other way just to fill the bars with pretty young boys, since it helped them sell more drinks to the older men.

We thought that our freedom with no responsibilities was justified because of our time spent with the doctor, even if the freedom was an illusion. We fantasized of the life we would make together as Aaron's anger gave way to his feelings of independence. Everything went well until freedom turned into something bad. His time in rehab hadn't done anything to help him stop using drugs. He'd just used the experience to ruin the doctor and find an excuse for us to get away.

Perhaps staying with the people who had introduced Aaron to heroin was an error. Brit and Robbie also liked to have fun and party but they had their limits. Neither one of them had the disposition to be addicted to anything other than attention. Somehow they both managed to pull off an ambivalent attitude toward drugs. They didn't have a favorite but they'd do whatever happened to be around. Robbie even kept a policy of *I don't pay for drugs*. They used drugs as a form of entertainment without the need to make a full commitment to the narcotic life. Maybe they were the definition of recreational users, if such a thing could exist. They maintained their day-to-day life and, unlike Aaron, neither would ever be a junkie.

I had no desire to try the drug. I'd watched its effects and they had terrified me. I couldn't understand how it had become the only place that Aaron wanted to spend his time. I took some measure of shelter in my constant attempt to understand, through observation, how the high felt for him. Beyond that nothing was under my control. There was enough chaos in our lives. I was trying to find some value or art within the chaos so I didn't want to let go of my observations; they were all I had. I was still a voyeur.

Brit brought the relapse on. She did it without considering that Aaron just couldn't taste it and walk away like she could. She set up the works for a Friday night before we were off to the show, but we never made it that far. Instead we sat in the studio while the three of them drifted in the world Aaron had described as like being on television and I watched the episode play out. I waited anxiously for their return. I sat silently, until Aaron's body started its journey away from the high. Again, I held him through the night sweats and shakes and I saw everything I ever needed to deter my own temptations. I couldn't imagine what trip could be worth the fire he had to walk through to return from it.

Brit and Robbie soon returned to the daylight world. They were a bit rough around the edges for a few days, but they returned.

This was not the case for Aaron. He was a true addict. He was a junkie. For him there was no way to leave behind what had been done or undone by the drug. There was always more out there to find. He slipped back into his addiction quickly and our dreams of making it on our own out in the real world gave way to his need for the high. He had passion for nothing but the next fix, and I followed along as his caretaker. Years before he had stood up for me and flattened James Marshall to the ground over an insult to my presumed sexuality. I saw it as the first time Aaron had expressed something that felt like love to me. I was worth defending. He'd wanted to be my protector. No one else in my life had ever taken a stand for me. I owed him my care even as his need for the drug caused him to lose sight of everything else.

"Shit, Caleb. You're burning up."

There was a touch of panic in Sonia's voice. I could hear her and feel her near me. I thought the room was pitch-black but my eyes had been closed with my face buried in a cluster of pillows. I felt her palm touch my forehead and it was cold and dry as she pressed it to the side of my face and then the back of my neck.

"How long have you been like this? How long has he been here?"

Her questions filled the room. I scarcely remembered that we were in Jack's house. Sonia looked for answers that no one had to give. Her panic then turned into anger. The only voice I could hear clearly was hers as Jack mumbled and shrugged in response to her queries. The lack of answers shifted her into rage. I could hear a familiar voice and knew it was Peter's. He told her to calm down and said that they should get me to the hospital. He begged her to stay calm and to call my father so that he would meet us at the hospital. Her anger grew even as Peter tried to keep things under control.

"Where the fuck is that piece of shit? How did he let him get this sick? Where the fuck is he?"

Her boots pounded across the floor and broke through my wheezing and the fever I couldn't feel much beyond. I heard her body slam against a door. It was the bathroom door, which was locked against her and shut everyone else out. The door that had left me alone in a strange bed with my chest heavy and short of breath. Fevered. I had bronchitis.

"Open the fucking door, Aaron!" She pounded with her fist as she screamed into the door frame. She tried turning the doorknob and again it failed to open, then she looked down at the lock. "Peter, go find me a screwdriver or something."

Sonia and Peter were both familiar with Jack's house and knew where to find things like screwdrivers, extra blankets, and towels. Jack had gone to the institute himself, ten years before the rest of us. Once he finished college and came back to D.C., he settled back into the neighborhood and opened the doors of his house to institute students for afternoon fun. Sonia and Peter had both spent time in the house before Aaron and I came along. The house was a safe haven for cute boys and Sonia had been welcomed there due to the company she kept. Her friends had always been the cutest of boys, to whom Jack gave joints and alcohol before he seduced them. Though Peter never fully gave in to Jack's attempts, it was the afternoons at his house that had caused Peter to break up with Sonia and leave the institute for Sandy Spring.

Aaron had remembered Jack when he realized that we needed someplace to stay. He knew I needed a bed to sleep in and warmth. He had to find someone who could see him through the next fix. He knew that he couldn't take care of me as I got sick and he could see that he had to find me someone more responsible than he was.

Jack had called Sonia and told her she needed to do something. She needed to get us out of his house. Aaron was shooting up in the bathroom and I looked like death in the bedroom. Our host screamed the details of it all into the phone as I buried my head into the darkness of the pillows. Sonia arrived with Peter and her anger swelled with the moments that passed without any of her questions answered. Jack just wanted us all out of his house and Aaron had locked himself in the bathroom.

She pulled my arm and forced me to sit up on the edge of the bed. She pushed my sweat-soaked hair away from my face and wiped the dampness from my forehead with the sleeve of her sweater. Then she unfolded a blanket and wrapped it around my shoulders.

"What the hell is wrong with him, Caleb? Why did he let you get this sick without doing anything for you? He's gonna kill you—, you must know this."

"I'm okay. We're okay. He's having a hard time." I tried to open my eyes and see her in front of me. The light blinded me. The room was spotted and out of focus. "He brought us here. He called you."

"Jack called me. Your boy wonder is in the bathroom, possibly OD'ing instead of helping you. You need to get away from him, Caleb. He's toast. You can't help him. He'll get you killed."

Peter returned with a screwdriver. The room was bright but had started to come into focus. I shivered beneath the blanket that Sonia had wrapped around my shoulders. Peter popped the lock with the screwdriver and pushed the bathroom door open. I squinted and I could see Aaron. He was stripped to the waist. His once beautiful body appeared gaunt and graying. He had his belt wrapped around his arm and a stream of blood ran down his bruised forearm. He had collapsed against the bathtub with eyes that gazed at the floor while his mouth hung open.

"Oh fuck." Peter moved quickly from the doorway and grabbed Aaron's chin in his hand.

I looked at the two of them and couldn't see the resemblance any longer. Aaron had wasted away as everything beautiful about him had been taken. The drugs had drained the warm golden color from his skin. His caramel eyes had grown bloodshot and yellowed. I squinted to be sure it was the two of them because I'd never seen them next to each other to make a true comparison, and now it was too late. Six months had erased the qualities they had shared. Aaron's transformation was so slow I hadn't realized the difference, but seeing them next to each other caused me to see it. I struggled to focus and couldn't look away, even as the tears started to come to my eyes.

"Sonia, I need some help with him. We need to get him awake and figure out what to do with him. And Caleb needs a doctor." Peter held Aaron's face with both hands as he moved his head from side to side and tried to look into his eyes. "He's fucked up, but we need to get him back."

Sonia joined the two of them in the bathroom. She spoke in a cold and loud way as she tried to get a response from Aaron. He was adrift in the high and wouldn't respond to her. I laid my head back down against the mattress and watched the three of them. Sonia stood and then I heard the rings of the shower curtain screech across the rod as the cold water sprayed from the showerhead into the tub. Peter lifted Aaron from the floor and stood him under the freezing-cold water. Aaron's eyes opened, then he looked at Sonia as the water startled him and made him alert.

"You're a bitch," he sneered and laughed at her.

She slapped him.

Peter closed the door.

I stared at the the closed door that kept from me whatever my two changed superstars had to say to each other. My chest heaved with the wheezing and heaviness of the bronchitis. I felt like I was sinking in the room; as if I were underwater with the sounds muffled. Then I could actually distinguish the sound of water running behind a closed door, as well as Aaron's insults, which were matched by Sonia's replies, spoken through clenched teeth. I heard nothing from Peter in the exchange. Everything faded gently to pitch-black again as I closed my eyes and drifted to sleep with short, fitful breaths.

accidents (problems)

Had I not gone to the emergency room I would never have gone back home. I was still a minor and the hospital needed my father's signature on a release to treat me. I had developed quite a case of bronchitis while Aaron and I had been out on our own. Though we had tried to find places to stay on the nights that were terribly cold, some nights we had wandered in the frigid dampness a long while before we found shelter. I tried to ignore the fevers and the coughing because I wanted to stay with Aaron. I was certain that we'd figure out a way to survive on our own. I was hopeful we'd get through the tough transition and find our fair measure of happiness. I pictured our cool jobs and apartment and our having the things we needed. Then we would look back on the homeless spell as the small price we had paid for our success. I hadn't thought of how we'd make it through if one of us got sick.

By the time my father arrived to sign the release at the hospital, my fever was so high that I was delirious. I'd forgotten that Peter and Sonia had found Aaron and me and I had no idea how my father had come into the picture. I thought that I had just left his home. The details were all jumbled and they confused me. The only thing I knew for sure was that I did not want to stay in the hospital. I cursed at the nurses and doctors until my fever broke and they told my father he had to take me home.

Aaron and I had made it on our own wits for two months. My family had let me wander off and had made no attempts to find me. I hadn't done a very good job of keeping up appearances, so perhaps it was better for them that I was gone. Out of sight, out of mind seemed to be the grown-up version of being seen and not heard. My absence meant they no longer had to see or explain my failings.

The time away gave me the opportunity to clear my head and get away from the memory of Dr. Moore. I now understood that he had quite possibly harmed Aaron and me over the years. But after our fathers had the doctor's license revoked, my father and I couldn't speak about my years in therapy. We both knew that he'd let it happen. Unable to do so himself, he'd put the doctor in charge of raising me.

Winters in Washington, D.C., were always sad, cold, and gray. My father had kept my apartment in the basement as I had left it and he made arrangements with the headmistress of my school for my return after the holidays to finish up my classes. I'd missed most of the term while Aaron and I were on the run but my father made a deal with the school for a sizable donation in exchange for a fast-tracked diploma.

Since I had been so ill from my bout with bronchitis my stepmother had agreed to let me stay with them in the main house until I felt better. It was, after all, the Christmas season, and my family performed all of their standard holiday bullshit productions. Christmas was a time of countless holiday parties in their Georgetown home. They hosted one cocktail bash after another. My stepmother had told all of their friends that I had just returned from my studies abroad as an exchange student. I was never certain what exactly I had studied, or where. Was it Smack 101, the Sleeping with Strangers Tutorial, or the graduate level of Back Room Survey? Surely, I'd seen a world of things that would shock polite company if I'd been asked, but I didn't argue with her public lies and excuses. I obeyed the house rule that children should be seen and not heard. If she said I had been abroad, I figured it was in my best interest to pretend that my French skills were improved by my travels. Her efforts to make excuses for me actually required more attention than her usual indifference or disdain.

Even Christmas itself was not a sacred day for my family. It had no more meaning to them than the engraved cards they sent to their list of the who's who of Washington society. Honoring the birth of Christ could and would be moved in order to suit our busy schedules. But, oddly enough, Christmas 1986 was celebrated on December 25. We could pretend to be just like a real family.

Aaron stayed with anyone he could and he refused to go back home while I returned to my father's house. No one had seen him until he turned up at my house one day between Christmas and New Year's Eve. The most recent time he'd spent on the street strung out and living by his wits had changed him further. The desperation made him weaker, and during that time the space between us had expanded.

We had spent so much time together since I was twelve that I missed him terribly. It had been weeks since I'd last seen him but even then the beautiful boy I loved was fading away. I felt that he and I had more reason to spend the holidays together than I had reasons to be with my family. With his scandal and our run he'd gotten me away from Dr. Moore and made me see how the doctor had manipulated our feelings for his own entertainment.

I felt weak from the illness and loneliness. This weakness was the cause of my first accident on Christmas Eve. They were always to be called accidents since no one in their right mind would ever try to kill themselves after his family had hosted one of the grandest holiday parties Washington had to offer.

I'd sat on top of the dryer in the laundry room and started by opening up my right wrist with a vertical line made with a box cutter blade. I didn't have a plan and the box cutter was the sharpest thing in the toolbox. It left a jagged line down the tendons and veins in my wrist. I'd meant to do both wrists but somehow I lost my nerve as I watched myself bleed from the first cut. The party had ended and the fire had settled to embers in the living room. My stepmother was in the kitchen, where she was making a list of the order of events for Christmas morning. Following house tradition, we would have breakfast and open our gifts in our pajamas for the photographer that was hired every year. Every detail was staged to give the appearance of perfection. I wore my Christmas pajamas as I sat on the dryer. They had been bought so that our whole family would match in the pictures, showing how happily we celebrated the season. The photograph would grace the Christmas cards my stepmother had planned for the following year. We would have been a picture of the ideal Georgetown family, but I dripped blood all over my snowflake trousers.

After I made the cut, I walked upstairs to the kitchen with my right arm hanging at my side. I stood next to the refrigerator and my stepmother looked up, asking me what it was that I *thought* I needed. I was silent but turned my right arm at an angle so that she could see the opening in my wrist as the blood started to drip to the floor. She looked from my wrist to her kitchen floor then to my face before she handed me a towel from the counter. She calmly walked to the foyer at the front of the house and put on her mink coat. She picked up her car keys and called to my father from the bottom of the stairs.

"Calvin, your son and I are going to the hospital." As she said this she opened the front door and motioned for me to come along with her.

The doctors at Georgetown University stitched my wrist up as my stepmother looked on. She told them it had been an accident. She said that I had reached into the toolbox and didn't see that the stripping blade was open. I nodded when the doctor asked me if her story was how it had actually happened. Then, even though the story was that it was an accident, a psychiatrist was sent in to speak to me. Apparently they were always accidents. The kinds of accidents that required you to stay in the hospital for seventy-two hours. They said it was for observation. My stepmother left the emergency room defeated that night. She had been unable to convince anyone that a suicide attempt on Christmas Eve was unintentional.

For seventy-two hours I had no visitors. I lay silently in bed alone. Three meals were brought to me each day. Injections assured that I would sleep and pills meant to balance my mood provided numbness for the hours that passed. It felt as though the cut remained wet under the gauze band around my wrist, with an itch that burned. I imagined that it had been stitched closed with silver thread. Silver like the wires of a robot, the walls of Warhol's Factory, or Andy's wigs.

The hospital psychiatrist visited me twice a day. The visits were a part of his required rounds for patients that were there for observation. I imagined that he and I were both robots. We were doing a job with his questions programmed and my answers delivered in a monotone.

Yes or no.

I was tired.

It had been an accident.

I was not depressed.

I didn't need to talk to another doctor.

If I ever felt I needed help I'd tell someone.

Yes.

Or no.

We each did our jobs for seventy-two hours.

We followed our programs.

Even though it had been an accident.

My father picked me up at the end of the holding time. He brought me the clothes my stepmother had picked out. I stuffed them in the plastic laundry bag and walked to his car in my pajamas. We both sat in the front seat; my father made no move to start the car. I stared ahead and through the windshield. For seventy-two hours he hadn't bothered to visit me. For three days, twice a day, the shrink had asked if my father had been in to see me. A yes-or-no question and I had to answer *no* every time it was asked. I shifted my eyes in my father's direction. He was looking at the gauze around my wrist. I pulled the sleeve of my sweater down to cover it and I felt the edges of the knotted sutures pressing into my wrist like needles. I thought of Aaron and needles. My father started the car and drove home without any words exchanged between us.

We never talked about the accident or the hours of observation. We arrived home and I saw that the door at the back of the closet that connected my apartment to my father's house was gone. The hinges had been removed and the door was now being stored in the garden shed. My father and stepmother left me alone in the basement apartment with no questions asked about the night of the holiday party. Instructions were given to the nanny and the maid to make sure I had food when I needed it and to check on me every few hours. I was under cautious supervision. The house was on a code red alert for accident awareness and prevention.

I sat at my desk and noticed a cassette tape on top of it. It had a label with my name written in black ballpoint ink on its side. It was Aaron's handwriting. He had been to the house and someone had let him into my apartment while I was away. Surely that meant he had been told there was an accident. I couldn't even put my hands on the tape because I didn't want to hear him.

My family's denial was accomplished with suspicious silence. After the accident my father kept track of my every move. If I left the house to go to the corner store for cigarettes, I was met with questions. If I didn't turn on the television or the stereo my quiet was queried. Meals missed were grounds for interrogation. I lived with their suspicions and caution. Certainly my accident had earned them. I received long looks that made my skin crawl whenever I looked in my father's direction. He gave those damp-eyed stares without words but I could feel the biggest question behind his gaze. We had never been able to talk to each other. I'd always felt that I was a mistake from his past that he and my stepmother had to endure. I was the thing that stood between my father and the picture-perfect life my stepmother wanted. We'd stopped communicating as I'd felt these things, and now we didn't seem to know each other well enough for him to ask me anything about the accident. When we should have talked we remained silent. But I could imagine his questions; I could see them in the way he looked at me.

He wanted to know the same thing the doctors had wanted to know. He wanted answers to the questions he couldn't bring himself to ask me. Did I want to be dead? Was I upset that I had failed? It wasn't an accident after all. I had wanted it and I had acted upon my want. With intent to harm myself I'd sat alone with a blade and cut. Afterward, my wrist was wrapped in tattered gauze as a reminder to all of us that there had been the intent. Those unasked questions about intent seemed to hang in the silence that buffered us.

Then the telephone broke the silence. It was a phone call for me on the last day of the year.

It was Sonia.

I had not seen or talked to Sonia since my first trip to the hospital for the bronchitis. She'd tried to call but I wasn't getting messages. My stepmother was trying to control which friends could contact me, and not many got through. Everyone was suspect. Even though Sonia had helped get me to the hospital when I was sick, I still didn't get her messages and I didn't call her. It was nothing insidious, I was just mute, accomplishing the silence my stepmother might have thought would make me normal, acceptable. The ring of the phone broke that silence, as I chose to answer it myself.

"We'll pick you up at ten." As always, Sonia didn't give options. She gave instructions. "You still have that Electromax ID, right?"

"Yeah. But I'm not sure I should be going out."

"Come on, Caleb. You can't stay at home. It's New Year's Eve. What are you going to do, watch Dick Clark? We'll be there at ten." She hung up before I could give her an excuse.

I sat at my desk and fumbled through my old photographs. I read through a few pages in my journal. I looked at my name scribbled on the cassette in the middle of my desk. I pulled the ID from my drawer and studied the snapshot and dates. It had my birthday on it with only the year changed, so 1965 was the only thing I had to remember. I put the fake into my wallet and climbed the stairs to break the silence with my father.

"I'm going out tonight. With Sonia."

I could tell his mind was nervous as it worked to find his strategy. I could sense his panic, and he chose his words carefully so he wouldn't say the wrong thing. He didn't want to risk my having another accident that was brought on by something he said.

"She's picking me up at ten. She thinks I should get out for New Year's. Do you really think I should sit in my room alone for another holiday?" I had seen his fear as he'd searched for his response. I played it against him before he could question me further.

"No. You should go out with your friends. New year. New start. Put the last year behind us. Do you need any money?"

He reached for his wallet and handed me a few bills. What my father may have lacked in emotions he always carried in currency. It was the way he dealt with all his relationships. If you got him anywhere near something he couldn't fix, the wallet would come out of his pocket. As I took the bills, I could see another thought pass through his head.

"Who else is going?"

I hadn't seen Aaron in weeks, but in my father's mind, Aaron was to blame for all my problems. Certainly my father regretted that he had handed me a large sum of cash before he knew whether or not it would go toward Aaron's problem.

"Just Sonia and Peter. I think we're staying at Sonia's after. I'll be home tomorrow."

"Good. You haven't seen Sonia in a while. You should have fun with your friends."

Sonia still had my father's favor, as she represented some chance at his son's being normal.

"Caleb, if you kids need a ride tonight, you can call and I'll have you picked up. Understood?"

"Yeah, Dad. I'm pretty sure we're staying at Sonia's though."

"Just be safe. Call me if you need to. No questions asked. Just be safe."

No questions asked.

Just be safe.

Without questions.

Sonia and Peter showed up a half hour early. Sonia worked my father over with her usual small talk and flattery and guaranteed him there was nothing to worry about. She promised him our evening was going to be nothing more than dinner, a bit of champagne, and a sleepover at her mother's place. It sounded like a perfectly normal evening, which seemed to ease my father's worries about a trip to the emergency room at some odd hour of New Year's Eve.

The evening actually consisted of our sneaking into the bars of Dupont Circle and Adams Morgan with our fakes. It was fueled by excessive amounts of alcohol and table dancing; we welcomed the New Year in the grandest style Sonia could muster.

"Shit, Caleb. Could you at least pull your sleeve down over that thing? You look like you're out on a day pass," Sonia scolded me about the gauze wristband as she handed me another Long Island iced tea.

"Leave it alone. He's with friends," Peter replied as he lit a cigarette.

"Yeah, Pete. With friends, but he doesn't have to look mental," she screamed over the beats that blasted from the nearby speakers in Madam's Organ as she lit a cigarette of her own. She puffed away but she didn't inhale.

Peter looked at her and nodded as he raised his glass for a toast.

"I'm glad you made it, Caleb."

I tipped my glass and nodded back. I set my drink on the table and pulled my sleeve down to cover the bandage as I tried to appease them both. I looked around the room at all the revelers and saw that half the crowd was our age, all of them in the bar with the same fakes from a Georgetown electronics store. They were drunk and carried on with desperation to make life in our town more interesting than its reputation for Brooks Brothers and policy work. I framed it all as though it were a film. I wished I had my movie camera, or even a Polaroid, with me. The lens was a shield that could keep me at a safe remove from everything. I missed the movies made in my basement with my superstars. My studio system had collapsed under the weight of our changes, but I had been happy as we built it all. We had made good films and should have made more, but I had let it go astray. I should have given them more direction. Or perhaps I should have stopped filming. In a movie it's just that easy. You press a button and everything stops. You kill the lights and the scene is over. You can tighten the shot and stop or you can traverse the landscape of his beautiful body and rest upon your favorite spot. Then you can stop there and never lose that beauty because you've captured it on film.

At midnight I wanted my camera more than ever. It was the moment of horns, jubilations, "Auld Lang Syne," toasts, and kisses. My camera would have saved me from being expected to participate. I stood and tried not to recoil from Sonia as she wished me a happy New Year with her kiss. The affection burned. When there's too much affection, you might be forced to deal with someone you love falling apart because of the noise of life. I just wanted to watch. The best of my films had no sound.

The revelry subsided and the crowd dwindled down. The three of us walked down Columbia Road to Sonia's apartment building. Her mother was asleep on the sofa with a glass of wine set on the floor near her dangling hand. She had the evening I wished I'd had. A night of television and solitude. She'd watched *American Bandstand* with no expectations or disappointments and had fallen asleep. Then her daughter came home and pulled an afghan from the back of the sofa and tucked her into safety and warmth.

"I'll sleep in my mother's room, you two can take my room," she whispered. "I'm beat. Good night, Peter. Good night, Caleb." She kissed us both on the cheeks and staggered down the hall to her mother's room.

Peter and I quietly stood as we looked around the room and then at each other. I shrugged my shoulders and smirked over the fact that Sonia had left us to our own devices with her mother passed out on the sofa.

"Wait here, I'll be right back. I have something I want to show you." Peter walked down the hallway to Sonia's room and returned with a boom box.

"I don't think we should wake her mom."

"It's okay, Caleb. We're going upstairs. Come on."

I followed Peter out of the apartment and up the service stairs all the way to the top. He pushed the door open and guided me out to the cold tarred rooftop. He took off one of his shoes and used it to prop the door open so we wouldn't be stranded outside in the cold. I walked to the ledge and saw the lights of the city as they spread in a panorama that twinkled before us.

Building code in Washington had always prohibited anything in the city from being taller than the Capitol or the Washington Monument. The effect created a panorama of white marble and green parks when seen from above. The town houses of Georgetown that I'd grown up among were packed side by side and stood no taller than three stories, but the density of them blocks the view most of the city enjoys. Our sheltered and affluent village of shops and cafés allowed me to ignore the Washington skyline while the rooftop of the Ontario gave me an expansive view.

Peter placed the boom box on the ledge and pressed play. "New Year's Day" by U2 blasted out of the speakers. It felt as though the song was carried with the lights of the D.C. night. Without a word from Peter I took it all in as I listened to the hard guitar work, steady drums, and strong rally call of Bono. My eyes watched headlights stream along the avenues alongside iconic buildings that were dramatically lit in a way that made them glow as if illuminated from within. The beauty was immense but the air was cold on the rooftop. I stuffed my hands into my pockets and shivered as I held my jaw tight and tried to keep my teeth from chattering.

Peter stepped closer to me from behind. He cupped the palms of his hands on my shoulders and rubbed up and down briskly, just as Aaron always did whenever I felt chilled around him. The memory caused my eyes to water before Peter broke the memory with his words.

"You wouldn't really want to have missed all of this, would you? One of these days you're going to figure yourself out. You'll figure out who you are. You'll make someone else happy then. You'll be a great boyfriend, someday."

With the gentle pressure of his palms he turned me to face him, then he leaned forward and kissed me gently on the lips. For the second time that night, I didn't respond to a kiss. I stood and stared at him through it.

All is quiet on New Year's Day. . . . I will begin again.

Nineteen eighty-seven started with a resolution in lyrics.

icons (art)

Aaron's cassette sat on my desk, where it remained untouched for well over a month. Seeing the tape there on the desk caused me a sense of failure, disappointment. He'd come to check on me and I was gone. Maybe he'd needed my help, but I hadn't been there for him. I imagined what seemed like a hundred ways in which I'd failed him.

I hadn't seen Aaron since the night at Jack's house. Even then, I didn't know him anymore. He'd changed. The drugs had made him into someone I did not and could not know. The tape might as well have been from a stranger, but it sat on the desk where every glance I cast on it kept my grief fresh. Otherwise I avoided the cassette until the day I placed it inside my Walkman and left my apartment.

I missed him. I couldn't bring myself to find him, but with the tape, at least I could hear his voice.

I took the Metro to the Hirshhorn Gallery. There I sat on the bench in front of Marilyn's lips and pressed play. I heard rough cuts of the Sex Pistols mixed with speed metal and New Jersey rock and roll. They were Aaron's sounds and not the electronic synthpop I liked. After I listened to a few songs his voice sliced through the squeal of electric guitars. He'd recorded his own words over one of his treasured tracks.

"I don't know how to talk to you any other way. Why? Why kill yourself and leave me here alone? You're the only one who knows me, what we've seen and who we've both been. You're the only one who accepts it all. Funny, but talking to this machine is no different than talking to you anymore. But you're not even you anymore, are you? You've changed yourself. Tried so hard to be him that there is no more you left, even your voice. Do you ever hear yourself? Can you still hear you, or is it all him? You had an accent when we met. Your soft accent is gone. You sound like a robot. I think I love you. Shit, I said it. I don't know why I feel like this. You can't die, because I think I'm in love with you, and it's not because of the stuff Elliot did. It's the stuff we did, or didn't do. I dunno. It's just this stuff I feel. Why did you do it? Did you think of me? Does this thing you've become feel anything? Are we all just stacks of Polaroids and some films to you? I love you and want us to be together. But now you're him, and not you. But I still want you—shit, that doesn't even make sense. I don't even know if you'll listen to this tape or watch any of our films. I just need to talk to you.

Don't die, don't leave me. I need you. You're the only thing I've got."

His voice cut suddenly and the chords blared their reverb along with the scream of uncontrolled vocals.

All I wanted was a Pepsi, just one Pepsi.

I laughed at the irony of the song. It was "Institutionalized" by Suicidal Tendencies.

Aaron couldn't have possibly listened to his own tape and left that song there. He'd obviously made the tape and left it for me before he could change his mind about leaving it. He needed to tell me those things in haste. He had felt my absence as I had felt his months before. But he had found some words for me while I'd stayed silent.

"Shit or get off the pot, darlin'."

So started my last lecture from Brit.

Brit had taken control of the role of Frank. Robbie's family problems back in Indiana had given her greater star power than she'd ever imagined. She encouraged Robbie to stay and help his family, but her motive was to keep the awesome limelight all to herself. She didn't need Robbie anymore, so she manipulated matters to keep him from returning and becoming Frank again. The starlet was cunning and getting rid of her presumed competition was just the beginning.

She'd moved in with some thirty-five-year-old lobbyist whom she had met at *Rocky*. Kyle had come with his fiancée and a few friends to see the show for the first time. He was a *Rocky Horror Picture Show* virgin, and he couldn't keep his eyes off of Ms. Brit that night. She was the star of the show and he thought she was the most beautiful girl he'd ever seen. After seeing the show for five weeks in a row, the lobbyist no longer had a fiancé or any old friends, and he appeared weekly in a gold Speedo as Rocky right beside Brit's Frank. Once again she had recast her life, landing herself an urban professional and banishing Robbie back to Indiana so she could put herself and Kyle under the theater lights.

You had to give the girl her due as she embraced change with all her being. It was so easy to believe the craziest of dreams whenever you were with her. She'd taken an otherwise straight, frat-boy lobbyist and turned him into a full-fledged *Rocky Horror* fairy in just five weeks. Then she got herself settled in as lady of the town house. In light of such grand accomplishments, she figured it was her turn to give me shit about my destiny.

"Why stick around here? The Factory is up in New York Shitty and it's clear that you and the boy wonder aren't ever gonna move to the suburbs and play house. The only thing you have going for you if you stay is a little mutual torture or trying to share the freak-show stage with me. I love you to death, darlin', but I'm not sure I can spare the spotlight."

"Why do you and Sonia always refer to him as the boy wonder?"

It seemed to be a joke I wasn't in on. The boy wonder was

Batman's sidekick and I certainly didn't feel very heroic. There was something else to it that I didn't see.

"Oh, darlin'. Because he is a man who will always be a boy. A curiosity, a wonder, and he looks at *you* in awe and wonder. You're his legend. An icon. Even when he doesn't know why or what it means he wonders about these feelings he has, and he doesn't think he wants to have them. It's wonder. You see? The boy wonder."

"He knows what his feelings mean. And I don't fill anyone with wonder."

I hated the fact that I always had to defend Aaron to Brit and Sonia. They both regarded him as a child. As though he was naive and not as sophisticated as the rest of us. They made an inner circle where they laughed at Aaron for his tenderness and innocence, mocking the qualities that made him lovable.

"Andy, baby. Aaron isn't going to get his shit together if the two of you are in the same town. He turned himself into a junkie to avoid the two of you. If you were ever interested in fucking the boy you should have done it a long time ago. He's been used so much now that it wouldn't be safe at all. If you leave and he really wants you, he'll have to clean himself up to make the trip. You're talented, baby. You belong where there is some beauty and art for you to be a part of."

I sat there in the dining room and stared up at the Matisse poster that hung on the wall. What Brit said about Aaron angered me and what she suggested about his being used and not being safe didn't make sense to me. I thought she had Aaron all wrong. She'd never given him a chance.

"What do you mean he wouldn't be safe?"

"Darlin', the boy gets fucked for drugs. Everyone knows it. He gives it up for drugs or for the cash to buy them. And he's stupid about it. He's got a rep, and I'm pretty sure if he's gone down that road he's sharing the needles, too."

Brit could be a gossip and she was flippant when she told me this. She knew I wouldn't want to believe it but she also knew if she was blunt about it, I wouldn't try to defend him. There just wasn't anything to be misunderstood when someone got that kind of reputation around town. In that respect we lived in a small Southern town—bad news traveled fast.

I stared up at the Matisse and had a sick feeling in my stomach. I was afraid that everything Brit had said about Aaron was true. I noticed that the Matisse was flipped and remembered something that I'd once read in a magazine. On a visit to Marilyn Monroe's apartment in New York, the writer Truman Capote had to point out to the actress that she had hung the Matisse upside down on her wall. Brit had worked hard at being Marilyn and had the style down to an art hanging. Even the Matisse was upside down. Brit's print was possibly hung that way by accident, but it seemed that she was exactly who she was meant to be. I sat, thinking through everything, and she allowed me silence. Aaron was a junkie and I still loved him. My only escape from our failures was to run away to New York, a city of art and life. I kept my eyes on the wall as I pondered.

"Your Matisse is upside down."

With that I stood from the table and walked out the front door. As I pulled the door closed I looked back and saw Brit. She stood there with her hands on her hips as she cocked her head to the side and considered the poster.

trains (solitude)

With a backpack, all the cash I'd taken from my savings account, and an American Express card I borrowed from my father's desk drawer, I left my disastrous past behind me to follow my Pop Art dreams. The miles, memories, and rails passed beneath the train.

I'd sat in the galleries day after day for a week after Brit had given me a talking to. I searched my heart for some reason to stay behind. Nothing surfaced, everything was in ruins. I made up my mind to leave home. I'd take my chances in the world of Pop.

As the train carried me north I listened to Aaron's cassette on my Walkman and flipped through the Polaroids I had saved to remember him by. They were snapshots of who he once was. I felt horrible for leaving him behind as I escaped the Beltway and followed a dream. I planned to send for him once I got on my feet. Aaron would like the city. He would ride the same train I had, then I'd show him around and he would be happy there. It wasn't the suburban splendor Brit had doubted we'd find anyway. It was my dream of something better.

I put the photos and the Walkman back into my pack and leaned my head against the window of the train. I watched the miles of cold winter landscape pass by and I let my regrets drift out of my mind, replaced by with hope and fears of about getting a fresh start in New York. I wondered if people just showed up at Warhol's Union Square offices and asked them if there was any work to do. I wondered what they might make of some kid just off the train, with all his belongings in a backpack, who wanted to be a part of their world.

I would have done anything. I'd have swept the floors at *Interview,* rinsed silk screens, and helped them in any way as long as I was allowed just to belong.

It wouldn't be my life in Georgetown with the confusion of my friends. The train tracks up to the city stretched forward and away from the past and its sadness. My dreams, hope, and potential were on that train with me, and with my beautiful future ahead, I rested against the cold glass of the window and drifted to sleep. But I could still hear Aaron's voice in my head, though the cassette no longer played.

Everything would be wonderful, everyone would be rich and beautiful. I would find my salvation once I connected to Andy Warhol and his world of Pop.

"Don't leave me. I need you. You're the only thing I've got."

death (emptiness)

It was February 22, 1987, when I arrived at Penn Station. Something felt out of place as I walked through the terminal and onto the street. The city seemed quieter than it should have been. There was a stillness to it that I didn't expect. A newspaper headline told me that something had been lost and an era had come to its end. Andy Warhol was dead. His philosophy didn't cover death because Andy didn't know anything about it. He would have preferred to say he went to Bloomingdale's.

Andy Warhol had gone to Bloomingdale's.

My icon was dead.

resurrection (living)

With my icon fallen I no longer had a goal. It seemed there was nowhere left where I would fit. The culture I had tried to find was gone and there was no one left for me to be. My appearance was now a skin I had to shed. I needed to find some way to keep my momentum, get away from death, and become myself. I felt people's eyes looking at me as I crept along the streets. I had the appearance of a ghost to them. I was a mockery of their loss instead of the emulation I'd intended. I was now in bad taste. The city wanted the original, not a hastily screened copy of the master.

I couldn't think clearly about anything. A sadness ran through my whole body and directly into the pit of my stomach. I was dazed and lost because no one I loved had ever died. Sure, a random Great-auntie So-and-So had died the year before but I hadn't really known her and I didn't go to her funeral. I'd gone to the funeral of a girl in the neighborhood who had been electrocuted by a fallen power line as she had walked on a path behind her grandmother's house in Takoma Park. I'd gone to that funeral because my stepmother thought it would look good for the girl's parents to have people there, but I hadn't really known her. She had just been a girl who lived a few houses over from me in our neighborhood.

I stopped at a barbershop near Washington Square and paid a Turkish man eight dollars to use his clippers and rid me of my blond mop. I didn't want to walk the streets as a ghost. I looked up into the mirror and didn't know the boy I saw. It was a trick of the eye. What I saw was an oddly placed image that didn't make sense to me. Nothing made sense to me.

I stayed at a youth hostel in Chelsea at night and wandered the streets during the day. On my second night at the hostel, my camera and Walkman were stolen out of my backpack while I slept. The man at the front desk didn't do anything to help me. He just pointed at a sign behind him that said they were not responsible for theft or loss. All of my Polaroids had been stolen along with my shoe box of memories. Aaron's cassette was gone. They had left my journal behind. I'd slept with the four hundred dollars I had rolled up in the crotch of my briefs, but the thieves had taken my dad's credit card out of my backpack's not-so-hidden pocket.

My great escape was fully realized as a failure.

With everything that I had left behind I couldn't turn back. I had no choice but to ask someone for help. I called the only person I knew who might be able to help me.

"Andy darlin'! How's the city?" Brit never was one for current events in the real world.

From a pay phone in Union Square, I poured my heart out to her about the three days I had been in NYC. I'd wandered the streets without an icon or a goal. I was lost in the honking horns, traffic, and lights. It was all a numbing blur to me. I sobbed into the phone as Brit patiently listened to everything I said before she tried to calm me.

"Darlin', I know that Kyle has to have some friends in the city. I'm going to call him at work now and see if we can get you some help. I need you to go someplace warm and get yourself some coffee and something to eat and call me back in an hour. Just give me an hour and we'll figure something out."

"Okay."

Those were the only two syllables I could choke through my sobs as I wiped my nose on the sleeve of my jacket. It was the resignation that I had nowhere else to go and nothing left that forced my two-syllable response to her instructions.

O. K.

"One hour, darlin'. Call collect if you have to."

Okay.

I put the phone back in its cradle and walked down the

street, looking into the storefronts. I stopped and dropped two dollars in quarters into a photo booth. When the black-and-white filmstrip dropped, I saw my shattered self. I took a pen from my pack and marked the date in the corner of the last of the four images and placed it in my journal. From a silver cart by the curb I bought a cup of coffee and a doughnut. As I glanced down the street I saw bins of books that wrapped around the corner in front of one of the buildings.

It was the Strand Bookstore. I entered and climbed the stairs to the second floor, where I flipped through bins of old magazines and remembrances of things I already missed. I looked up at the clock and realized I had only ten minutes left to walk up the street to the nearest pay phone and call Brit back. I bounded down the stairs and back out onto to the street. I walked one block north to Union Square and picked up the receiver to make the collect call.

"Andy, darling! Did you get something to eat? Stay warm?"

"Yeah. You have any luck yet?"

"Kyle has a friend there in the Village. He worked down here at the World Bank for a while, but now he's up doing that Wall Street thing. You know the type? Makes his money moving money or something. Kyle called him and asked if he could help you out for a while. He said he could meet you at four o'clock on the steps in Union Square. Do you know where that is?"

"Yeah, I'm looking at them right now. Does this friend have a name or any other distinguishing features I should be on the lookout for?"

"Sergio. He's Colombian or something. Expect pinstripes. He's Wall Street." Brit laughed at her own observation.

"I'll be on the lookout. Dark and businesslike. And Brit. Thanks."

"No problem, darlin'. I hope it works out."

"Yeah, thanks."

I hung up the phone with a few hours to kill before it would be time to spot a Colombian stockbroker in the middle of Union Square. I wandered the neighborhood as I listened to the traffic and watched the people pass through Union Square as they made their passage from downtown to uptown. I walked up to Times Square and stood in the center, looking at the lights all around me. They were as iconic as any canvas. But it was a constantly changing canvas of bulbs. As I stood in the center of it all I was no one. I was unnoticed, invisible, and anonymous.

I walked back down the avenue and found myself again at the doors of the Strand. I'd been drawn back to the art books on the second floor which, brought me comfort. Just like my lunches at the day school, the large volumes full of paintings and photographs gave me an escape from myself. I sat in the stacks and studied the images in the books. I passed the hours with Avedon, Brassaï, and Caravaggio. They all made darker beauty than anything Pop had. It was a kind of darkness that seemed familiar to me. I checked the sticker on a copy of Andy Warhol's *America*. The price was twelve dollars. I wasn't certain of how long my four hundred dollars would hold out in the city, but I walked down to the cashier and bought the book anyway. It was a chronicle of the life I'd just missed. I put it in my pack and looked at the clock on the wall. It was ten minutes to four so I walked up the street and took a seat at the center of the Union Square steps. I was the only thing other than the statues that wasn't moving. Surely Sergio would be able to spot me as I sat watching the blur of citizens pass me. There was nothing Pop in the blur of workday suits on a Tuesday afternoon.

"Andy?" a low, accented voice questioned me.

"Sergio?"

"Yes. You're Kyle's friend?"

"Yeah. But it's actually Caleb." I stood up and shook his hand. "Brit calls me Andy, but it's Caleb."

"Oh. That's right, she renames people. Kyle was Kevin before Ms. Brit got ahold of him." Sergio smiled as he shook my hand.

He was typical Wall Street. Just as Brit had said, he was a thirty-something South American business type in pinstripes and wingtips. He told me that he was actually twenty-nine, which made him twelve years older than me. He was well dressed and wore a stylish haircut slicked back with gel. Everything about him was typical of a status quo young urban professional—scrubbed and perfumed like all the other suits who passed through the park.

"So, Caleb. I live over in the West Village. We can walk from here. If you're hungry we can grab a bite to eat on the way."

I nodded my head. He pointed our way across the square and we walked down Broadway until we picked up Eighth Street toward the Village. We stopped at a small Chinese restaurant along the way and ordered dim sum.

Sergio told me about himself. He said he was from Colombia and that some of his family lived in Miami. He'd gone to college in London and had started work with the World Bank while he was there. It was that job that had taken him on to Washington, where he'd met Kyle at one of the World Bank's mixers. After living in London, he found Washington to be dull, so once he had a lead on a finance job in New York he shipped his things up and started a new life in the city. He spoke of life before his arrival in NYC with nostalgia, but like me he had spent his life looking for something more than what he already had. He'd come to the city to escape his boredom elsewhere. I'd come to follow a dream and escape the drama back home. But my dream had died and I felt like I hadn't escaped anything.

"Caleb, why does Brit call you Andy?"

No one had ever asked that question before. Everyone back home had just accepted it as a fact. But then, back home the answer was obvious just by looking at me. With my blond mop of hair, pale skin, and style of dress I had worked hard to copy the image of Andy ever since my first summer at the Corcoran. The emulation had lasted until I felt that my imitation had become a disrespect to the legend. I had shed my years of careful study like a costume that had grown too hot to stand. For eight bucks, I'd left it all behind on the floor of a barbershop.

"When we were younger, my friends all thought I looked like Andy Warhol."

It seemed a simple explanation. I didn't want to share the whole story with Sergio. I didn't want to have to be Andy Warhol anymore.

"Really? That's crazy." Sergio looked at me for a moment and laughed as he popped another dumpling into his mouth. "You're much better-looking than that."

"Thanks," I muttered, focusing on my chopstick grip.

We finished our dumplings and walked through the Village. Everything there was new to me. I lingered in front of the shop windows and street vendors. Anything could be had in the city, but I hadn't taken notice of these things my first few days. I'd been numb with what I thought was the worst sadness I had ever felt. I'd walked the streets like a zombie and everything had been a blur. I had stopped breathing while I drifted along in grief. So when I walked the streets of Greenwich Village with Sergio, I took notice of all the little things for the first time.

It was a tour of the everyday things like shop windows, bookstores, and groceries that usually went unnoticed. I could see the shelves and tables of goods as though they were art. It was the same world the iconic soup cans had come from.

Sergio was patient with me and didn't rush me along the sidewalk. When I lingered he stood in the background, where he waited and watched. He allowed me to take it all in. He seemed like a nice enough guy. It was his patience that comforted me. He made me feel that I wasn't alone in the city. With him that afternoon, I thought that I had a safe place to stay so I could figure out what to do and where to go now that my dream had died. He seemed kind.

Sergio's apartment was a walkup. We climbed three flights of stairs from the street to the apartment. Sergio turned the key in the lock and held the door open for me. He lived in a small one-bedroom decorated in a sleek decor of stark black and white. I'd heard that this was the preferred style of the Wall Street go-getters, so half the apartments in the city probably looked the same way. With black metal, glass, and the requisite leather sofa, it was typical. I stood in the doorway and looked over the place from end to end with a sweeping glance. Sergio shut and locked the door behind me, then turned and pressed me hard against the wall as he forced his hand down the front of my jeans and looked me dead in my eyes.

"So, Caleb. You need a place to stay and I like to have a bit of fun. This could be a good arrangement for you. You understand?"

I understood. Beneath his kindness was another motive. I wondered if Brit had understood that I would have to exchange favors for his help. I glanced at the locks on the door and back into his eyes, the eyes that waited for an answer from me. I was alone in the city with nowhere to go and had an offer to trade myself for a place to stay. I looked at the door and back into his eyes.

"Yes, I can try."

"Good. Let's go take a shower."

A smirk spread across his face as he eased back from holding me to the wall. I didn't know what the smirk meant. I didn't know if he considered it a victory, a conquest, or if he was attracted to me.

I wasn't attracted to him. I just needed a place to stay. I thought of the times Aaron must have made the same deal for drugs, and shuddered.

We had an arrangement that wasn't a relationship. At the start of it I tried to convince myself that I would eventually like him. He paid the rent and bought me things. To an outsider it would have appeared that I was kept. I'd been a teenage boy right off the train from D.C. who was now dressed in the trendiest of suits and had plenty of time on my hands. I fucked a stockbroker every morning in order to keep up appearances.

It was an arrangement without affection. I knew my rent was paid in full. I needed a place to stay and he liked sex. On the best of days I didn't really like him and on the worst of days he repulsed me. He didn't seem to care about any of that. I had the libido of a seventeen-year-old with a morning erection and that was all he wanted of me. We slept in the same bed but were certainly never a couple.

The sex became a routine in the shower on mornings before he left for work, although he certainly took me any other time he felt like it. Though I started out inexperienced, he eagerly instructed me on his preferences for asphyxiation and penetration.

Whether I got off wasn't important as long as I was gripping his throat while I rammed my cock into him. As he taught me how to do this, I was afraid I would hurt him. Before that I'd never had sex with a guy and I didn't know what to do. This caused him to laugh at me, and his laughter quickly replaced my fear of hurting him with disgust. Then I tried to be so rough that he wouldn't want me, but it only encouraged him, as the rougher I tried to be the more he seemed to enjoy himself. I'd rarely imagined sex at all, and now I was trained that it was better when violent.

The only sex I'd had so far in my life were those three awkward attempts with Sonia and the sex with Sergio that gave me a place to live. With those examples, I wasn't sure I liked sex at all. Fucking felt like a job to me.

In the shower I tried to imagine my beautiful friends, my superstars. I tried to replace the disgust I felt toward Sergio with happy memories of Aaron, Brit, and Sonia. They had been the most beautiful people I had ever known but imagining them didn't help me like I wanted it to. Yes, I had affection for them and I liked watching them. I'd had a voyeuristic affair from a safe place behind the camera, but I didn't think about fucking any of them. I watched them like I looked at paintings of lips, soup cans, and soda bottles.

Voyeurism was more rewarding than sex.

While Sergio was at work, I passed my time by exploring the city as I tried to sort out what to do with myself. I took sanctuary in the art museums and the galleries. As they'd done before, the paintings helped me think and brought me comfort. The city itself was an ever-evolving canvas with its always changing billboards and the blinking lights of Times Square. The foot traffic of Union Square provided countless hours of people watching with the dance of young professional New York as my entertainment. Everyone scurried around me without taking notice of the vibrant everyday art they lived. I'd sit there, just yards away from the Warhol offices on Union Square, their beautiful past now shuttered in. The mirror that was Andy Warhol didn't reflect the city's colors upon itself anymore. The skies, pinstripes, concrete, and towers were all a wash of gray.

After our morning showers, Sergio would leave me some cash for the day. It was never enough for a train ticket or a flight. I was certain he knew better than to leave enough money behind to give me any independence. But he left enough for coffee, magazines, and the occasional entry to the Guggenheim or MoMA. It seemed to me that everything in the city cost something—until I found the library.

The library on Fifth Avenue, with its entry guarded by the legendary stone lions, provided me with the same type of sanctuary I had found in the galleries. There was a world of security and comfort found in the stacks of books and research materials. I was granted monastic silence and reverence with entry there, but I found the faintest sadness in the silence as I sat at tables in the reading rooms and remembered fondly the library at the day school. I thumbed my way through books that reminded me of my favorite subjects in school. Art, literature, and French. The things I had pretended to study as Aaron had worked in his sketchbooks.

I daydreamed of the past, hoping to look up from pages of conjugation and see his warm brown eyes looking across the table. My hope was never realized. All I ever saw was the thinking city of graduate students and intellectuals with their heads buried in the vast collection of information. I sat alongside the homeless people and paid respect to the silence of the space in exchange for its shelter. I watched the tourists who marveled at the Beaux Arts structure. But I never saw his eyes or his smile or his scrunched eyebrows hunched over a sketchbook when I looked for them there. I just had my regrets and daydreams.

I couldn't check out any of the books. The resources of the public library were reserved for residents of the city. I wasn't a resident, I was just the morning fuck of one, so there were no bills in my name, no signed lease, and no driver's license. I had none of the proof that I needed to show that I should have been entitled to a New York City Public Library card. I was a phantom dweller of the city. I was just another boy who had followed a dream and had seen the dream shattered. I wandered in and out of the crowds of residents. My rent was paid under streams of running water seven days a week, yet nothing made me worthy of a simple library card.

I was invisible just as I had always been invisible. It was only through imitation that I had ever been seen. Without the mask or the illusion, Caleb Watson was again invisible. I needed something to give me value. It was something I'd never considered before as I'd had no experience. I needed a job.

"But I take care of you. Anyway, what can you do?"

I hated the conversations I had to have with Sergio. My interests were always too common for him. In his eyes, the music I liked was bad and my tastes in art were unrefined. He thought I had lived a sheltered life and I had no sense of style. He even hated the green striped soap I brought home from the drugstore, though he didn't know that it was the only thing that got me through our morning ritual. He had no interest in anything about me, but his low opinion of me was tossed around with words like *What can you do?* The only thing he liked about me was the size of my cock and the fact that it was his to use in exchange for the shelter he provided me.

"I can get a job in some kind of store. Maybe a gallery?"

The look he gave me told me what he thought of my idea. What a common job it would be.

"Sure. If any of them will have you. Why not?"

"I need to borrow some money to get a few shirts. I'll pay you back as soon as I get my first check."

"I buy you plenty of shirts. Better shirts than most of the idiots that work in retail. What do you need with shirts?"

"I can't get a real job in some designer shirt, Sergio. I need something normal. Something like everyone else wears."

"You know, you should just fuck them for the job you want. Then you wouldn't even need a shirt."

He pulled me toward him by the waist of my jeans. As he unfastened my belt and tugged at the buttons he looked me in the eyes and sneered. I glared at him as he slid his hand past the elastic of my briefs. Without a word I looked coldly into his dark eyes as I willed myself to not get hard for him. I resented and resisted him.

"Fine. We'll go to the Gap and get you some boring shirts."

He pulled me down on top of him on his bed as he pushed my jeans and briefs to the floor. I'd once read in *The Philosophy* that relationships were about exchanges. *I'll pay you if you pay me.*

I got through it all with some more of *The Philosophy. So what.* I got through much of my life in the city that way.

A legend dies.

So what.

Can't get a library card.

So what.

Fuck someone you despise.

So what.

I hadn't imagined it could actually be that simple, but throughout the years Andy had never failed me.

Miserable? Far from home and those you love?

So what.

I documented my time in New York as Warhol often did, with self-portraits in the photo booths. For two dollars in change I'd get strips of instant film delivered via a slot. In the four poses in black and white from booths scattered throughout the city, I recorded my time. I built a collection of photo strips showing the city's effect on me as I grew older, rougher, and more mature in a few months' time. The pictures showed my transition as well as my misery. My eyes had lost their twinkle, and I'd become tired, cold, and hollow. I hadn't found a way to turn my experience in the city around. My journey had turned me into an empty shell. I was one of those people you ran into and wondered, *What had he been before he gave up?*

The *so what*s had eaten away at me.

Every morning started with a job hunt, but no one wanted to hire a seventeen-year-old with no experience at anything. I didn't understand how a person could feel all washed up before they had really begun anything. Life in the city seemed a cruel joke.

After hunting, I passed my time in the library. I cruised the stacks for anything that caught my eye. Whatever I wanted to learn about that day I'd pick up, then I would sit in the reading room as the hours passed immersed in art, languages, history, and social sciences. It was a liberal arts education at my own pace.

Late in the afternoon I would start my walk home down Fifth Avenue to Union Square and over to the Village. I'd stop at the Strand to browse through the art books before I went back to the walkup to deal with Sergio. Our interactions had evolved from our morning rituals to his patronizing me as his evening entertainment.

At the Strand I found comfort. The managers and clerks there learned my name and they started to let me know when something new and of interest to me would hit the shelves. It was a familiar comfort that reminded me of my early days with Dr. Moore, the care people took to share things with me. In a city full of strangers, the books were my friends and the Strand was the place where all of my friends lived and I found where feeling of acceptance and understanding.

"Caleb, what do you do all day?" Jerry, the manager of the art books section, asked as he pulled a Brassaï book from the shelf of rare editions.

"I hang out at the library and read."

I carefully turned the pages of the book. I studied the extraordinary plates of light and dark. It was the finest edition of Brassaï's *Paris by Night* prints I'd seen. They were his most brilliant art. On film he'd captured secret back rooms, smoke-filled jazz clubs, brothels, and bars where boys kissed boys. It was decadent and romantic art.

"Are you a student?"

"No. Not anymore."

"Are you from the city?"

"No, I'm from D.C."

"Do you live alone?"

"No. I live with this guy. He works on Wall Street. It's complicated—we have an arrangement."

I was at ease in the bookshop. I'd never talked to anyone about my life in the city before. Jerry raised an eyebrow at the word *arrangement*.

"Do you work?"

"No. No one seems to think I can do anything. No experience. No one wants me."

"Are you kidding me? You're a smart kid."

He straightened the stacks of books and postcards on the desk. Jerry seemed annoyed or flustered by my admission that no one would hire me. He seemed to take it personally. He propped his elbows on the desk, leaned forward, and spoke in a hushed tone.

"I think I have a few shifts open here in the art section. It's only part—time and the pay sucks, but it would be a job. Do you think that would work out for you?"

A job. He offered me a job in one of the few places I'd ever felt safe. A place where I was surrounded by beautiful books. Without hesitation I took the offer.

"Yes. What do I have to do? When do I start?"

"Great! Come by tomorrow and we'll do some paperwork and put you on the schedule. I'll train you myself and we'll try to find you some more hours soon."

I had a job in a beautiful place that gave me a paycheck. With my own paycheck I would get some independence from Sergio and his moods.

It was my first job.

learning (adult)

I thrived in the bookstore. I learned everything about it quickly. Everyone there was impressed by my knowledge of the art section and my memory of which artists we held in our extensive collection. I knew where to find things the minute that customers asked. Jerry soon found me extra hours here and there and I covered shifts whenever the other employees wanted to have some time off. The pay wasn't great, so Sergio and I still had our arrangement, but what I earned at the bookshop was mine to keep and save.

I read everything that I found in the bins at the front of the store as well as the books that publishers sent to the store for the staff. Books were practically free to me and the stacks that filled our apartment annoyed the hell out of Sergio, which secretly delighted me. I covered extra shifts on the weekends so that I didn't have to spend more hours in the apartment despising him. My job at the Strand was the best thing that had ever happened to me. I was respected. I was good at something and people thought that I was smart. I was happy when I was surrounded by beautiful books.

"I can't believe you don't want to go to college."

Jerry had started to mention college every time we worked together. With his nonstop encouragement, it was like having a big brother or an uncle who brought it up at every holiday-dinner.

"I don't know what I'd go for, Jerry. They have tests and stuff. I never really liked school much as a kid anyway."

"That's ridiculous. You're one of the smartest people I've ever met. You absorb things. You don't even have to learn. You absorb. You should at least apply to a few and then figure it out when you get there."

"But I have to take tests to get in. I don't know test stuff."

"Caleb, trust me. You already know everything you need to know for those tests. Just take them. Apply to a few schools and you'll see."

"I dunno."

Jerry didn't take my excuses for very long. He arranged for me to take entrance exams and scheduled me off on a Saturday to sit for them. He had my shift covered, paid my exam fee, and took me to the library at NYU for the test. He sat in the hall and waited for me to finish. Then he took me out to dinner afterward.

"Have you thought of any universities?"

It was a conversation I should have been having with someone else. It was a father-and-son talk. I'd never had one of those before.

"Shouldn't I wait to see if I even passed the test?"

"You have to write essays, fill out forms for college applications. By the time you get that stuff together you'll have your test scores. Pick a few schools. They have catalogs at the library."

I picked only one school. It was a school I was familiar with and I was certain it was a long shot. I figured I'd get a rejection letter from them and then I'd be able to get Jerry to back off for a while. One school, one essay, and one application. I was certain I wouldn't get in. It seemed impossible but soon I was accepted. The school was Georgetown University.

I returned to D.C. with no more than I had left with: a backpack and a few personal belongings. Jerry had walked me to the train station to see me off. Sergio thought I was going to work and wouldn't realize I'd left until he got home from the office and waited in vain for my return to his apartment, still littered with my books.

I didn't call anyone to let them know I was back in D.C. Since I was enrolled at the university on my own merits, I received a modest scholarship that was supplemented by the work-study program. I lived in the Copley dorm as a normal, eighteen-year-old, anonymous freshman. I even took my meals in the cafeteria on the student meal plan. I stacked and ordered textbooks in the bookstore of the student center in exchange for tuition while I studied art history, literature, philosophy, and theology, in classrooms now. No one there knew anything of my life before or how I'd spent my previous months in New York. All of my professors challenged me to do my best in all my subjects. They were impressed with my work and never asked questions about where I'd come from.

As with my job at the Strand, in college I was respected, seen as intelligent, and I was pleased. I wrote letters to Jerry and told him everything, thanking him for pressuring me to go to college.

One day on Wisconsin Avenue, near the punk store Commander Salamander, I passed Aaron. He looked drawn and ill, his hair limp and greasy around a face that held vacant eyes. I knew he was still using heroin or something worse. I saw the bruises that covered his arms while all of his athletic form had been lost. He had wasted away. I called out, but he walked right past me like he didn't know me, or perhaps he was too high to see me. I turned and watched him walk down the avenue until I lost him in the crowd. I never saw him again. It was as if that day on Wisconsin Avenue I had been a ghost. I heard the news of his overdose later. His parents didn't have a funeral for him. What was left of my once beautiful friend was cremated and sent back to his mother in New Jersey.

I settled into college life as the fall leaves covered the steps of my dorm. I studied hard and worked in the bookstore without taking time to get to know any of the other students. It was just easier to be contented alone. There was no chaos in being alone.

"Caleb?" A familiar voice called from the grass on the quad as I walked the path to Copley. I turned and saw Peter. He stood from his spot on the grass and gathered his books. "Are you enrolled here?"

"Hi. Yeah, I just started this fall."

"I heard you were in New York?"

"Yeah. That didn't work out."

"Does Sonia know you're back here?"

"No, I didn't really tell anyone. My dad doesn't even know I'm back here."

"Not even Aaron?"

"Aaron's gone."

Peter didn't question Aaron's whereabouts any further. I didn't know if he knew what I meant by *gone*. Aaron's family hadn't even run an obituary in the *Post*. The only reason I had found out about his overdose was because I'd called his father's house. I had gotten up the nerve to try to talk to Aaron and thought Chuck might know where I could find him. I called a month after I had passed Aaron on the street. Chuck haltingly told me that Aaron had overdosed alone in a motel room up Route 1 in Virginia. It was two days before his body was discovered. I should have called sooner. I didn't know if Chuck had ever told the story to anyone but me and it wasn't my story to share so I didn't say anything else about it to Peter.

"Well, Sonia is in Paris. She and her mother moved back there over the summer. I think she started university there this fall. Hey, do you want to go get a coffee?"

"I can't right now. I have a lecture in twenty. I was just going to my dorm to get some notes. Another time?"

"Sure. Whenever you're free. I'd like to catch up some more. Are you in the student directory?"

"I think so. But you can usually find me at the bookstore. I work there."

"Caleb Watson has a real job?"

Peter smiled at his question. No one at Georgetown has to work. Privileged kids get into schools like that, so work makes you an outcast.

"Yeah. Weird, huh? I gotta go. Find me for coffee. Tomorrow. I finish my shift at the bookstore at two."

travel (air)

After I'd learned that Sonia was in Paris, I set up a meeting with my academic adviser. Together we cross-referenced my credits and made arrangements for my transfer to a university in Paris. My adviser was sensitive to the troubles I'd had over the course of a life in Washington and thought the move would be the best thing for me. She secured the letters of recommendation necessary from the university's fine arts and literature department heads and the American University of Paris took me with no questions asked.

Peter and I met for coffee a few times before I left for Paris. We spent our afternoons together over caffeine and conversation about my time in New York, the bookstore, and art. When deep in conversation, Peter would always throw me off track with a compliment. After everything I'd been through, I couldn't believe that he could still see anything on which to compliment me. Yet he always did. Peter had the same direct and honest quality that Sonia had.

"You've changed a lot. The things you've done have made you a bit rougher. But you've still got those pretty, stormy eyes."

A sly grin spread across his face as he stabbed the ice in his glass with his straw and looked directly at me.

I didn't mention Paris to him; I hadn't even called Sonia to tell her I was coming. I planned to call her from the airport when I got there. In just two days I'd be an ocean away and only my academic adviser and the university in Paris knew anything about my plans. I hadn't even packed. My plan was to just take a backpack with my journal, two pairs of Levi's, a sweater, my Docs, my passport, and a new start away from my hometown, though Washington was a town that never felt like home to me.

I swirled the coffee in my cup, took the last sip, and looked across the table at Peter. He smiled at me and raised his eyebrows in the middle as some sort of question or playful expression when I looked at him. The effect was straight-up dork and made me laugh. It made me think of Aaron.

"Hey, my room is over in Copley, why don't you come over and hang out?" I offered.

I would leave two days from that question. It's true that Peter and I had kissed a few times over the years. I remembered the time we had been on the roof of Sonia's apartment building on New Year's Eve. We still didn't talk about that night. I had come through a hard time and he had been kind to me, which I appreciated. I could tell that Peter liked me, though I had never thought of him in that way. Before that day in the coffee shop, I had never seen his resemblance to Aaron so clearly. He reminded me of a healthier, happy Aaron. Then I remembered something he'd said to me on the roof. He had told me I was going to be a great boyfriend once I figured out who I was. That was right before I went to New York. It hadn't even been a full year earlier, but it felt like a lifetime had already passed.

"Are you sure?"

It was both a question and his insecure response. He'd always played and flirted with me but I don't think he ever expected me to reciprocate. I was taking the challenge of that flirtation and had asked him back to my dorm to act upon it. I no longer felt like the confused kid on the roof. Too much had happened since then.

"Yeah, Pete. I'm sure."

"We don't have to do anything."

"Peter, I fucked somebody for an apartment for six months. I think I understand that we don't have to do anything," With that I pushed my chair back from the table and swung my backpack over my shoulder. "Are we going?"

Peter stumbled over his backpack as he rushed to his feet. He looked down at the book-stuffed obstacle, then he glanced over at me and did the eyebrow thing again. I smirked at him while I shook my head. He reached down, grabbed the straps, and tossed the bag over his shoulder. We walked across the student union toward the doors and he tried to affect a cool swagger, but it wasn't very convincing. We each hit the lock bar on separate doors at the same time and they swung open to a path on the quad with the winter gray sky spread out overhead.

As we walked across the quad, I told Peter about my roommate situation. Ironically, my roommate, Mark, was in many ways everything I could have been. The two of us were like a case study of the different paths life could take. We were both born to Texans involved in politics, survivors of divorce, prep-school educated, and Ivy-university ascended. Yet somewhere along the way we ended up opposites. Mark was a burnout who split his time between going the gym, getting drunk on bottle after bottle of NyQuil, and lighting Gonesh cone incense in our dorm room. As far as room-mates go, he wasn't so bad, since he was passed out cold most of the time and our room always seemed to smell like a Krishna temple. Still, I felt the need to warn Peter about him. You wouldn't want to spring Mark on someone without warning, even if he was passed out at three in the afternoon.

I don't even know why I cared. Two days later I'd be gone, and Mark would fail out of school before the end of the following term. Rumor says that he finished his poli-sci degree at some state school back in Texas before he returned to Washington as a legislative aide to some Republican senator who was known for hate speeches and shady business deals.

Peter listened to everything I said, his backpack slung over his shoulder; he nodded in acknowledgment and offered an *uh-huh* or a laugh now and then. Every time I looked over at him I could see that he was watching me intently and that he looked away from me only to keep his footing. I glanced at him and for the briefest of moments, I saw the old Aaron, as though he walked the path with me. Maybe I was forcing the similarities, but they were still there, at least in my eyes, much like the multiple images of a silk screen: the same but different.

We entered Copley and took the main stairs up, bounding two at a time to the third floor. When we reached the door to my room, I turned to give Peter one last warning about Mark. I assured him I was pretty sure my roommate was out cold. He nodded and silently mouthed an *okay* before I opened the door to the smell of fresh incense and the sounds of Depeche Mode playing low on the stereo. I glanced over at our bunks and found my roommate asleep on my bunk, the bottom one. I pushed the door open and held it in place with my shoulder as I turned to Peter with one finger to my lips in a silent shush. He nodded and smiled as I guided him into the room with my free hand on his shoulder. I closed the door gently and pointed toward the bathroom door. I followed him as he walked in and set his backpack on the floor below the sink. I tossed my backpack down next to his, then I closed and locked the door, leaving Mark to his New Wave and NyQuil intoxication.

I leaned my back against the door as I studied Peter for a moment. I couldn't make myself really see him, couldn't shake the vision I'd had earlier. I just saw Aaron, his hands jammed into the pockets of his corduroy trousers as he rocked on his heels, with his eyebrows scrunched upward and a half smile on his face. I stared at him and tried to adjust my vision to see Peter there in front of me. My gaze seemed to make him nervous. With almost a year of experience behind me our roles had reversed. I wasn't a naive little boy anymore and it seemed that made Peter more timid than he used to be with me.

"Hi," he sheepishly replied to the way I watched him.

"Hello."

With my gaze still focused on his form, I moved toward him until we were face-to-face and our eyes locked. He leaned forward and kissed me gently on the lips with his eyes closed, while mine remained open. I watched him lean forward into the kiss. In silence he could have been Aaron.

"You wanna take a shower?" I asked when he pulled back from the kiss.

A smile spread across his face as he responded simply yet enthusiastically.

"Sure."

I pulled my sweater and T-shirt over my head and tossed them on the floor. I opened the door to the shower stall and turned the spigots, mostly hot with just enough cold to keep us from being scalded. I checked the temperature with my hand, unbuttoned the first two buttons of my jeans, and turned back to look at Peter.

He had stripped down to plaid boxers and gym socks, and all of his clothes were neatly folded on top of the toilet tank. I couldn't help but laugh at him.

"What?" His brow scrunched again with the question.

"I don't think you're gonna need the socks."

I popped the last two buttons on my jeans and slid my white briefs and jeans to the floor, stepped out of my shoes and socks, and let it all collapse behind me as I stepped into the shower. With the hot water beating down on my shoulders, I motioned for Peter to join me with a tilt of my head. He lifted one foot after the other, tugged the gym socks off his feet, then pushed his boxers to the floor before he stepped into the shower stall and pulled the door closed behind him. He stood in front of me. We were face-to-face as my blue eyes locked with his golden brown ones. He smiled nervously as he tried not to break the eye contact. Then he gently put his hands on my hips as the drizzle of the water bounced off my shoulders, splattered his face, and glistened through the dense fur covering his chest. Aaron didn't have as much hair on his chest the last time I'd filmed him. Perhaps it had gotten more dense while I'd been away. Peter could look just like Aaron if he didn't speak too much. The only difference I could sense was in the mildest inflection of his accent. Peter had an accent that carried clues of growing up the youngest in his Greek household, not the New Jersey brawn Aaron had.

Sonia had commented on this resemblance when we first met her at the institute. I'd always dismissed it. Through my eyes Aaron had no equal. Even now he had no equal. Peter was just a substitute, but the resemblance caused my cock to get hard.

My time with Sergio had conditioned me to separate the act of sex from actual desire, but once I'd gotten the routine down I wondered what it would feel like when you actually wanted it. I couldn't have Aaron and I wondered if I'd have enjoyed it if I did. Peter was my only means to approximate the experience. I realized the desire was there, though the object was gone.

"What do you want to do?" Again his eyebrows scrunched into that look but his voice was not the one I wanted to hear.

"I need you to turn around," I said in a low tone. "And stop talking."

He glanced down for a moment before he looked back into my eyes, biting his bottom lip nervously. Without a word he turned around as I had asked. I placed the palms of my hands at his hips and gently pulled him back toward me as I pushed my cock into him. Peter drew in a breath as I pushed as deep as I could. He responded with a whimper and a gasp but he didn't utter a word. He could have been Aaron.

When I walked with Peter across the campus to his room in New South Hall, he had asked if we could see more of each other. I didn't mention Paris and I didn't tell him I would be leaving two days later. I just shrugged my shoulders and told him that it would be great to see him again.

"I knew you'd make a great boyfriend someday. I'm glad you figured yourself out." He leaned forward to kiss me in the doorway of New South.

Had I figured myself out? I fucked Peter because he looked like a dead boy I could never touch again. I was planning on leaving and he was making plans to see more of me. I had nothing figured out aside from the fact that I wouldn't see Peter again after that day.

I couldn't tell him about Paris any more than I could tell him the shower was about me and Aaron. As he bounded up the stairs and out of sight I thought of Aaron ascending up into the sky on stairs, off to heaven. With a smile on my face I headed down the hill toward M Street.

I'd seen flyers attached to newspaper boxes all over town the previous week. With Warholian multiplicity, the black-and-white photocopies on pink paper of the image of Marilyn Monroe smoking a cigar, with the word *Biological* followed by a question mark beneath the image, were everywhere. An address at the bottom of the flyer was for a bar in Dupont Circle and the cigar-smoking Marilyn was Brit. It seemed she was the emcee for a beauty pageant. I walked down M Street and headed east toward Dupont. I cut along the Rock Creek path to P Street, up to Connecticut Avenue, and half a block to the front door of the bar on the flyer.

I knew the place. I'd snuck into Rascal's a few times

over the years. I walked through the door and saw that nothing about the place had changed. It was still the same dive that Aaron, Sonia, and I used to get into with our fakes after we'd snuck out for the night. The same weary bartenders in rooms of gray-washed walls. The space was filled by dim lights, throbbing bass beats, drag queens, pinball machines in the hallway, and a heavy air of desperation. Rascal's could guarantee its patrons at least one hookup any time of day with its three floors of entertainment. There were transvestites on the ground floor, pornography on the second, and go-go boys on the third. I'd run into one of the Transylvanians on the street one day and had learned that while I was away Aaron had worked a brief stint on the third floor, but was fired when some of the older gentlemen complained about track marks on his arms. I never confirmed the rumor and I honestly didn't want to know if it was true or not. I'd heard a few secondhand accounts of what Aaron may or may not have done in the last six months of his life and I filled in the details from what I had seen before I went to New York. None of it was the way I wanted to remember him. I wanted to remember him as Peter ascending the stairs.

I wandered the bar to kill time. I took the stairs to the third floor and worked my way back down to the ground floor for the show. I stopped on each floor for a drink to take the edge off. I had whiskey and cola. The drink was a habit I'd picked up to deal with my life with Sergio. I'd drink just enough to numb myself.

Suddenly a loud blast of cabaret-style music announced that the show was about to begin. I leaned against the back wall of the bar in the shadows and looked toward the painted plywood stage. The starlet climbed to the center beneath the floodlights with her silver sequins awash in harsh pink light. There stood the emcee of the night's festivities.

I was right, it was Brit. She traded lowbrow barbs with the crowd and encouraged speculation as to what equipment the contestants had wrapped into their gowns and swimsuits. The contest consisted of marginal lip-synching to Top 40 songs and a swimsuit competition. It was an opportunity for the desperate drunks to guess who was the real girl and who wasn't. Had Brit been a real girl, she would have been a performance artist or an actress on the stage, maybe even the screen. But, since she wasn't, the happy-hour drag show at a dive bar was part of her waning star in Washington, a descent into nightlife obscurity. I remained in the shadows and watched her. She was just going through the motions, throwing around a series of cliché one-liners and collecting her dollar tips from the audience as she lip-synched old Marlene Dietrich numbers.

The lights were garish, as somehow the pink gels were not doing their normal trick of softening things. The starlet that I had so admired for her courage and tenacity now appeared desperate and petty. Had less than a year away opened my eyes and caused me to see things so differently, or were they always this way? I couldn't decide.

I sank deeper into the shadows as Brit worked the room

and introduced the next performer. As soon as she slipped into the DJ booth, I snuck out the back door and into the alleyway.

I tried to remember our nights out in Georgetown at the Key Theatre and Au Pied. I tried to remember the images in cans of film back at my father's house. I thought of Marilyn as Andy had seen her. He had preserved the best of her to share with the world. Marilyn endured; she was frozen in time. Since no one had to witness her downfall under garish lights, they hadn't seen her turn from a starlet to something desperate and sad. Andy had preserved her as an icon.

I walked up the alleyway and back up the avenues to Georgetown. I couldn't turn around to say good-bye to Brit. It was as though the starlet I had loved had already faded and I didn't want to see or know more of what she was becoming.

I stopped at the newsstand and bought a stack of post-cards. They were of my favorite spots in Washington: the Jefferson Memorial, Dumbarton Oaks, cherry blossoms in bloom, the Hirshhorn Sculpture Garden, the Marilyn mural on Connecticut Avenue, and the pandas at the zoo.

I sat alone on the famous steps as the moon reflected in the water passing under Key Bridge. I watched the headlights of the suburban nightlife stream into Georgetown and wrote my good-byes to everyone.

To my father, Peter, Elliot Moore, Brit, and finally Aaron.

On my last day in Washington I went to my church—the galleries. Since Andy's death all of the Pop pieces had been pulled from their archives and put on display. Where once only one or two Warhols hung, the walls were now covered with them. The modern collections had become an impromptu retrospective. A tribute. The curators and collectors inside the Beltway had scrambled to scoop up whatever images had remained on the market and hung them on whatever wall space they could rest a plaque on.

The lips took center stage at the Hirshhorn.

I sat on the bench in front of the two panels just as I had years before. I was entranced by the beautiful repetition of Marilyn Monroe's lips on pink and white as an iconic image, frozen and immortal. It was the singular painting that had fueled my childhood dreams.

The lips held all of the beauty and secrets that I'd emulated and pursued since adolescence. I'd used them as inspiration for my own dreams of perfection and sensuality. I had tried to collect them in varied forms. I'd been the voyeur. I'd imagined those I loved as superstars. I had tried to immortalize them in my films, snapshots, and cassettes. Their own perfection played out in the basement apartment of my father's town house.

It was art, but we hadn't gotten away with it.

I looked at the lips with my eyes cast on the sadness. Marilyn knew sadness and the lips looked back at me knowing our shared secrets. We both knew love and loss. But here, Marilyn's lips knew the adoration of becoming an icon, equal to being religious art to the boy I no longer was.

I stood from the bench and rode the escalator down to the basement and entered the men's room. I stood at the sinks and studied myself in the mirror. It had been almost six years since the world of Pop Art had given direction to my life. I splashed cold water on my face and took a long hard look at myself. I was no longer smaller than everyone else; puberty had grown me to the same size as my friends. For the first time since that summer at the Corcoran, my hair was its natural dishwater blond and cut short. I'd finally started growing a beard, so I looked scruffy since I could never remember to take the time for shaving. And my eyes, the icy blue ones that Peter described as stormy, no longer gave away the shy little boy who wanted to be Andy Warhol. He'd grown up and found there was no magical, silver Factory to run away to.

I pulled a paper towel from the dispenser and wiped the water from the face I'd never bothered to see before, then I turned and walked out of the Hirshhorn. It was the last time I would see Marilyn's lips. Caleb Watson wasn't going to be Andy Warhol. I needed to create a life, an identity of my own.

The next morning I grabbed my pack and walked out of my Copley dorm. I left a note behind for Mark, giving him everything I had left behind in our room. I took the Prospect steps down to M Street and headed to Rigg's Bank, where I closed out my meager savings account in exchange for traveler's checks, then I walked down to the Four Seasons and caught a shuttle to Dulles Airport. I checked my pockets for my passport once every five minutes. After I passed through the metal detectors, I took the tram out to the international concourse and had two hours to kill before my overnight flight. I looked at the photo strips in my journal and studied the changes I'd undergone in NYC. I was curious what Sonia would think of me. Once she'd learned that I was at Georgetown she had sent a few letters. I hadn't been able to find any words to return as I sorted through my plans to go to Paris. I wanted my arrival to be a surprise. I skimmed over her letters as I sat and wondered if Peter had tried to call me or if Mark had found my note yet. Everything that was my life seemed to come down to a few letters, notes, and a phone I wasn't in my dorm room to answer.

The Air France desk agent roused me from my musings with the intercom. I had successfully passed the hours with queries and photo strips. As I walked the Jetway with my pack slung over my shoulder, cold air blew in the gap between it and the aircraft. I stepped over the line of cold air and onto the plane. For a moment I considered whether boarding the aircraft counted as my first moment of being an expat. I knew that my step from the edge of the Jetway would be the last time I would be in the United States for a long while. When I looked out the window, I could see the sun setting on the landscape of suburban Virginia, but I couldn't see any of the city from the airport. The next sunlight I would see would be on the other side of the Atlantic after my overnight flight. I imagined myself in France from the moment I boarded that plane.

Once seated, I pulled the French dictionary from my pack. Over the years French had been my only passion outside of art. I returned to it as I flipped through the pages and read random words, making a game of creating imaginary conversations with whatever words I happened to land on. Certain words carried better emotional value in French for me. They were the words that the English language couldn't convey with the same depth of feeling. As I flipped through the dictionary, I found one such word. My heart knew it well.

Tristesse.

It was sadness. Though the literal translation didn't even touch the feeling that it actually carried in French. It was the most intense sadness imaginable, the kind that emanated from my heart and ran a course throughout my body. *Tristesse* was the word you could use to describe the feelings that made you empty, lonely, and starved. The sadness that came from a sense of loss when you knew you had once been happy and full. But then found yourself lost and longing.

On the jet, I slept off and on for seven hours. I knew that all I felt was namable only in the language of my destination, but my heart knew the word throughout.

Tristesse.

Halfway across the Atlantic I dreamed of a night at Dumbarton Oaks under a canopy of wisteria. I was at the

Arbor Terrace with my friends. The dream was in vivid color and all of my friends were at their most beautiful. Sonia was a smoky-eyed punk rock princess. Brit a beautiful starlet, my very own Marilyn. Aaron, a sculpture of perfect masculine beauty with warmth, life, and the smell of green striped soap. The image of Aaron was fuzzy, though. One moment it was Aaron and then at the next glance it was Peter. My mind had trouble separating them in the dream. Even their words mixed.

I think I love you. I knew you'd figure yourself out one of these days.

I'd once heard that all characters in a dream are aspects of yourself. Certainly the people you love influence who you become, but the voices in the dream were real to me. I felt warmth, safety, and love, and I didn't want to wake. I wanted the dream to pull me down to it and keep me there with all its beauty. Half-conscious in the dream, I told each of them that I didn't want to leave them.

One by one they said that I never would. Brit touched my cheek and told me I could be anything. Peter, with his optimistic and goofy grin, flirted with me. Aaron's tender eyes gazed into mine as he rubbed my shoulders to warm me. Then there was Sonia.

"Mesdames et messieurs, bonjour! Nous arriverons au Paris Charles de Gaulle en quelques moments."

The attendant announced our arrival and stirred me from my reverie. I could see the edges of the Parisian morning sun as it struck the drawn shade. I tried to close my eyes and fight my way back into the beauty of my friends in the Arbor Terrace, but it was all gone. I couldn't return. It was the past. The *tristesse* returned and flowed from my heart out to my fingertips as I opened the shade.

Our descent was already quite low. I'd kept the shade pulled during my opportunity to see the village of Paris from the air. As the flat fields of the suburbs raced beneath the plane in the morning light, the cabin lights blinked to a dim setting with all the power being channeled for the landing. I felt the first touch of the rear wheels to the edge of the runway and the sadness lifted a fraction as the aircraft slowed its speed. I closed my eyes and tried again to recapture the dream but there was nothing there. My eyes opened. I looked out the window and found the Aéroport Charles de Gaulle on the horizon. My first glimpse of the future was in front of me while my past had been left 3,839 air miles behind on the other side of the ocean. I put my hand to my chest, feeling for my passport in my pocket. The flight attendants spoke only in French once on the ground. *Bienvenue.* I paid enough attention to the announcements to hear myself welcomed home. I pulled my pack filled with the last of my belongings from under the seat in front of me. I unbuckled the seat belt and waited for the moment that the aircraft came to a full stop so I could walk down the Jetway with the hope that the sadness would not follow me.

Aside from a few questions as to why I had so little luggage and a student visa, I breezed through customs. I passed through the doorway past the *Police Nationale* and found an information kiosk and currency exchange station. I got directions to the Metro and a fifty-dollar traveler's check exchanged for a pocketful of French francs. I had a handful of brightly colored bills and gold-toned coins that held no more meaning to me then than the play money you get with board games. I laughed at the thought that Warhol had said in *The Philosophy* that American greenbacks were the most beautifully designed currency in the world. How could he have thought so with the kaleidoscope of color on the simplest French bills?

I made my way to the Metro station and found a pay phone. I opened my journal to the page I had written the number on when Peter gave it to me. The number that was about to ring in a small Paris apartment, a new home I would share. I hadn't been able to actually talk to Sonia as the months had passed; I didn't even know where to start. But I knew the friendship we had would always be there. True friends stay with you no matter the distance or time that separates you from them. I knew that we had that. We always had. I'd traveled thousands of miles from our hometown for the friendship and love I felt certain of.

I looked at my watch and thumbed through my collection of photo strips. Would she even recognize me anymore? I had changed so much. I had become something rougher and older in such a short time. I had finally caught up to the physical maturity of my friends. *Tristesse* had accelerated my youth. It showed in the photo strips. I looked at my watch again. I dropped coins into the pay phone and hoped that I wasn't waking her at 8:30 a.m. I listened carefully to the new ring, the French telecom's low beep, as though even the phone had an accent. Would she answer?

"*Allo?*"

"Hello, Sonia?"

"Caleb? Hello. What time is it there?" Her voice was smoother than I remembered it.

"Um, half past eight in the morning,"

"That's what time it is here. Where are you?"

"Roissy Metro Station."

There was a pause on her end of the line.

"In Paris? You should have called. I would have come to the airport. Do you need me to come get you?"

"It's fine. I think I can manage on the Metro. We have one back home." It was so good to hear her voice again. It had been almost a year since I'd heard her voice. The sound of her so near lifted the sadness a bit more. "Where should I take the train to? I'll come to you."

"Saint-Germain-des-Prés. I'll meet you on the corner of Saint-Germain and Rue de Rennes. Are you sure you don't need me to come out to Roissy?"

"I'm sure I can manage it. How long should it take me?"

"About an hour. You can read the Metro maps, right?"

"They look like silk-screen paintings. I'm sure I can figure them out." I laughed into the phone.

"Good point. I'll see you in an hour. Caleb, I can't wait to see you, darling."

Sadness lifted more as I set the phone back in its cradle

and walked toward the Metro map, finding my route into the city. I took Roissy to Les Halles, changed trains, and continued on to Saint-Germain-des-Prés. It was all drawn simply enough in the brightly colored lines of the Paris Metro map.

As I traveled the hour from the outskirts into the heart of the city, I absorbed everything I could on the Metro, with its impromptu puppet shows at the front of the cars between the stations, the musicians moving from car to car, and all manner of street performers giving their shows in the few moments between the sliding doors. The great style of the morning commute, but done here with much more joie de vivre than I'd seen from New York buskers. The city of fashion and beautiful people. Paris was a centuries-old city of youthful beauty and style. I studied every detail as I had often studied paintings in the galleries. I tried to eavesdrop on conversations. I realized I would have to make myself a quick study because my language skills were fine as a hobby an ocean away but the street language of the city was new to me. I had only six more stops to Sonia.

Saint-Germain-des-Prés is the hub of the Left Bank. I climbed the stairs from the tunnel to the street. The bustling streets were full of Parisians starting the day. I tightened the straps of my pack and looked up and down the avenue. A beautiful woman with a wild mane of blond curls approached me. She was just as stylish as the rest of the city and she stopped in front of me and cupped her hand at the nape of my neck.

It was Sonia.

The sadness swelled in me in that moment. I looked into her eyes and saw that the storm that was once there had been calmed. I started to cry for the first time since Andy's death. The first tears I'd shed for Aaron, the best friend and most beautiful boy I'd ever known. The love of my life, and I'd never found a way to tell him. All the years I should have said something, but what we had wasn't something we talked about.

"Pouquoi est-tu triste, mon amour?"

Why are you sad, my love? A voice of genuine concern, asking in order to find a way to help me. Her words were an act of love. I felt as though the tears would never stop. I looked back into her eyes without their storm and wondered if my new life would temper my storm.

"It's just us now." I choked the words through the tears.

She pulled me forward and brushed her fingers through my short hair as she looked into my tear-glazed eyes. She tried to calm the storm as her lips gently kissed mine. She now had the same tenderness with me that Aaron once had.

"I always thought it was just us."

Her words softened my tears.

"I fucked Peter." A guilty confession.

"It's about time someone did."

She smiled coyly as she rubbed the back of my head with her fingertips. She cleared the tears from my eyes with the corner of her scarf. The softest silk wiped away pain, grief, and secrets.

Sadness loosened its grip and feeling returned to me.

Sonia and I had always had a most true and accepting love between us. I could feel something that I had lost during my first days in New York. I could feel hope. I knew again that my heart was still beating. I'd loved my friends with the deepest and most private parts of myself. I'd loved their tenderness, beauty, and all the things we never said to each other. I'd loved them in different ways, but I had loved them all. I was finally certain of that love.

A full beating heart is the greatest happiness.

It is unconditional and boundless.

I found myself standing motionless in awe. I was on another continent. I was not my past but I was with the only person who knew or understood that past. She knew what I was capable of. She knew that I could just turn and walk out. But she was standing right here with me anyway.

I wouldn't be the guy who walked out again.

I had wandered to a place I would make home.

I looked into Sonia's eyes. They were calm and full of love.

"I love you, Sonia."

I'd never said it before, to any of them. From the other side of the lens and watching them in our adventures, I had felt the emotion and never voiced the words. I wouldn't let another one of them slip away without ever the words. I repeated once more.

"Oh, Caleb. I know you do." With her fingers still laced through the hair at the back of my head she kissed me softly again. "We should get something to eat; they have sandwiches and stuff at the drugstore." She moved her hand from the back of my head and took my hand in hers as she led me down the Boulevard Saint-Germain.

As I walked along, I made a silent resolve to myself that I would always walk along and never again walk out.

I glanced at our reflections in the glass of the storefronts. The thoughts I had of the life ahead of us made me happy. She knew all that would make me *triste* from time to time, the sadness from the past that shadowed me, but together in a new city with a different language we would find some happiness.

As we came to the corner I noticed the name stenciled on the glass: DRUGSTORE PUBLICIS. The ashtray on the desk in Elliot Moore's office had come from a Drugstore Publicis. It seemed so far behind me, but the hours and years in his office had put me here. The years ahead would always have reminders of who I had been. The Warhol exhibits would circle the globe. Sonia would take me to see how the Parisian kids celebrated with *The Rocky Horror Picture Show*—glitter, glamour, and the time warp with a French accent. All of it made up just fragments of who I was becoming. Like the brushstrokes on a painting, not a silks creen print but a delicately layered painting.

The life lesson I'd needed wasn't in Pop; it was in *Rocky Horror*.

Don't dream it, be it.

I pulled open the door to the drugstore and as we stood in the doorway Sonia turned to look at me with a question on her lips. The same question she asked every time we'd gone out in the past. The one I was always happy to answer with a *yes,* just for the pleasure of her company. I laughed and answered her before she could even speak.

"Yes, don't worry about it. I have a bit of cash."

Acknowledgments

Without the support of a strong network of friends and loved ones *Pop Salvation* may have never come to be. My heartfelt thanks go out to all those who helped me along the way, not only with the work but with their efforts to remind me that along with the work I still need to enjoy the beauty of every day. Special thanks to Susan Henderson and all the guests and readers of Litpark.com for great words of encouragement.

With great affection and endless gratitude to Alexander Chee, Juliet deWal, Josh Kilmer-Purcell, Robert Westfield, and Heather McElhatton for their guidance and support when it came time to find a home for my first novel. To Christina Winton and Megan DiLullo for enduring me through the worst parts of the whole process of getting the story onto the page; those two women in my life deserve a medal of some kind. Thanks to Lois Sandusky for giving me great feedback straight to the emotional core of the story on one of the first reads.

I'm forever indebted to Stephanie Fraser for not only loving the characters as much as I do but for pushing me to be the best writer I can be, and to Carrie Kania for getting the unsolicited draft into Stephanie's hands in the first place. To Isaac Eamer, for keeping me safe and secure through some of the most challenging bouts of writing and revision. You sheltered my heart and soul and I'll treasure that, for always.

And last, to Mom and Dad—I wish you were still here to share the experience. I miss you both every day.

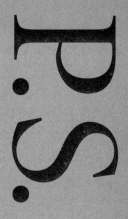

About the author

About the book

Insights,
Interviews
& More ...

Read on

Meet Lance Reynald

Lance Reynald was born October 16, 1970. He is the only son of his parents' brief marriage. Raised by his father and stepmother in Washington, D.C., he spent his childhood years shuffled through several private schools in the D.C. area, always finding himself on the outside of the grammar school social scene. He briefly attended classes at the Capitol Hill Arts Workshop and the Corcoran College of Art + Design and then attended liberal arts classes at Georgetown University, taking particular interest in theology and literature while giving his

The author, age 4

father the vague hope that the
whole endeavor might lead
back to some interest in politics.
(No dice.) Impatient with the
structure of academia, he
supported himself over the
years with a series of odd jobs.
He has sold chocolates and fetish
apparel; worked as a photo stylist,
makeup artist, barista, stock boy,
art framer, telemarketer, hair
designer, cosmetics product
consultant, freelance interviewer,
and contributing writer for
online zines; and may even ▸

rank as the worst waiter you've ever had (that gig lasted only two weeks—it was a pathetic attempt at hospitality services).

He has traveled extensively and is most comfortable with one carry-on bag and a valid passport, stylishly vagabonding. Over the years he has briefly set the bag down in New York, Paris, Madrid, Montreal, Santa Fe, Boulder, Toronto, and, for the moment, Portland, Oregon.

Reynald has an affinity for vanilla lattes; dirty martinis; the works of Faulkner, Kerouac, and Burroughs; the smell of imported cigarettes in fine woolens; the photography of Doisneau and Brassaï; and what some regard as the worst taste in early '80s Britpop.

He also likes Krylon black spray paint in an assortment of finishes. When he is not busy writing, his housemates remark, you can always tell when he's home by the sound of the power drill going in a never-ending quest for more suitable decor. ～

Red-Eye Flights and Heartbreaking Work

I'VE ALWAYS BEEN FASCINATED by the life of Andy Warhol and his humble beginnings as a sickly child of immigrant Pittsburghers who was able to transform himself into one of the most recognizable celebrities in the art world. His persona was as much a work of Pop Art as any screen image of a soup can. Andy really did it: he took something everyday and often ignored and made it into an icon.

I knew from the book's beginning that I needed my characters to know and appreciate this fact. I wanted them to find the art within themselves through experimentation and emulation.

Initially I floundered around with the idea a bit, finding the Warholian influence too broad. Then I took a long hard look at Caleb. How would he find himself?

It came to me as I flipped through *From A to B and Back* ▸

5

Again. Caleb would know the book well. He would adopt *The Philosophy* as his own. *The Philosophy* would serve as a self-help book to weather adolescence.

Then came research and travel. I sought out the canvases and films that would shape Caleb's thoughts. I sat in galleries, reminding myself to try to see things as a teenage boy would. I also read more closely through *From A to B and Back Again*, taking the time to dog-ear the pages and highlight the areas that might give a boy like Caleb hope. In addition to that research work, there were a few red-eye flights to NYC so I could just spend a few days at a time walking the avenues, exploring the Strand, and imagining how all of it would feel to a seventeen-year-old runaway in the late '80s. The work was at times heartbreaking. These were not easy characters to walk with. But by letting them grow on

66 Then came research and travel. I sought out the canvases and films that would shape Caleb's thoughts. I sat in galleries, reminding myself to try to see things as a teenage boy would. 99

their own, I found out more about them than I'd ever imagined possible. The surprise was the fact that the whole journey helped me get to know myself a bit better. ∾

The *Pop Salvation* Playlist

I ALWAYS HAVE MUSIC PLAYING as I write. Some of it fits neatly into the era while some of it just feels right. I make playlists that fit the story. At one point I think the *Pop Salvation* playlist topped out at more than six hundred songs.

Here is a sample of the playlist for the rough draft.

"Our House"—Madness
"It Must Be Love"—Madness
"Love Affair"—Erasure
"Désenchantée"—Mylène Farmer
"La Vie en Rose"—
    Mylène Dietrich
"Come On Eileen"—
    Dexys Midnight Runners
"New Year's Day"—U2
"Satellite of Love"—Lou Reed
"Stay"—Shakespeare's Sister
"Tainted Love" (7" Single)—
    Soft Cell
"Only You"—Yaz
"The Love Cats"—The Cure
"Lullaby"—Book of Love
"Love Affair"—Erasure
"Pretty Boys and Pretty Girls"—
    Book of Love

"Kooler Than Jesus" (Edit)—
     My Life with the Thrill Kill Kult
"Every Day Is Halloween"—
     Ministry
"Love Missile F1–11"—
     Sigue Sigue Sputnik
"One Day I'll Fly Away"—
     Nicole Kidman
"My Heart . . . So Blue"—Erasure
"No One Is to Blame"—
     Howard Jones
"New York, New York"—
     Nina Hagen
"Haunted When the Minutes
     Drag"—Love and Rockets
"Slave to the Rhythm"—
     Grace Jones
"There Is a Light"—
     Robert Schipul
"Closer"—Nine Inch Nails
"Home"—Duncan Sheik

     Then in revisions it changed
a bit and was refined to include
these in the background:

"Don't Panic"—Coldplay
"I Feel It All"—Feist
"Paralyzer"—Finger Eleven
"You Keep Me Hangin' On"—
     Kim Wilde
"I Want Candy"—
     Bow Wow Wow ▶

"Stop Me"—Mark Ronson
    featuring Daniel Merriweather
"Relax"—
    Frankie Goes to Hollywood
"Language Is a Virus"—
    Laurie Anderson
"Sex with Strangers"—
    Marianne Faithfull
"I'm So Beautiful"—Divine
"You Think You're a Man"—
    Divine
"Hungry Like the Wolf"—
    Duran Duran
"Planet Earth"—Duran Duran

And naturally, *The Rocky Horror Picture Show* was watched a handful of times during the whole process. A few dozen, in fact. ⌒

Everyone Can Use a Philosophy

ALONG THE WAY of discovering Caleb, I found things within the Warhol philosophy that I've applied in my life, with some modifications to bring them into the digital age. Andy was a workhorse in his approach to art, so I can't even imagine what he'd be doing with the vastness of social networking. But I've tried to adopt the Silver Factory approach in the basement of an old Craftsman house in Portland, and it seems to keep me busy enough.

My roomies are great at indulging me and living with a makeshift photo/video set and studio in the house. And ever since my best friend moved in, we've filled our time brainstorming this zine idea with which I've become obsessed. I'm fascinated by the whole zine scene and the fact that it still thrives in the age of blogs. These are amazing little works of art that people ▶

> ❝ I've tried to adopt the Silver Factory approach in the basement of an old Craftsman house in Portland, and it seems to keep me busy enough. ❞

tirelessly reproduce down at
the local copy center. The main
branch of the Portland library
has a whole section of these little
things. There is really brilliant
art going on in that world, and
I can pass countless hours at
the shelves, inspired by it all.

I'm not sure what I'm going to
do with the obsession yet. It just
feels like a medium I'd like to
give a whirl—and I'm sure
Andy would approve. ∽

Additional Inspiration

I LOVE THE DRESDEN DOLLS. If you don't know them yet, go look them up. Punk Cabaret is Freedom!

I don't really watch much television anymore, but the *Iconoclasts* series on Sundance is great. My favorite part is how the artists featured are universally driven by the fact that the art they make is the only thing they can do in their lives. There is a certainty and conviction to their pursuits, much like the way I feel about writing. Seeing them explain it on a screen is pretty inspiring.

To really dig into the life of Andy Warhol, there is no better documentary out there than Ric Burns's *Andy Warhol*. The four-hour documentary, part of PBS's *American Masters* series, really captures it all with beauty and sensitivity.

The best actor portrayal of Andy Warhol in a film goes hands down to David Bowie in Julian Schnabel's *Basquiat*.

I love the Kid Robot store. ▶

Plastic art toys blow my mind in much the same way that Pop Art does. Check them out at kidrobot.com.

And make a trip to Pittsburgh. The Warhol Museum can't be missed (warhol.org). ∽

About "That Bag"

ONE OF THE QUESTIONS I most frequently get about my bio concerns a certain bag kept packed near the door.

Yup, it's true. I'm happiest when vagabonding but I loathe baggage claim, so I managed to get all the travel essentials down to one bag. For the record, it is a Chrome Messenger bag.

Contents follow:

Laptop—Apple 13" Macbook. Black. ▸

iPod—There are always tunes.
Shoes—Converse One Star high-
tops. Black.
Pants—American Apparel
trousers. Black.
Shirt—White oxford.
Necktie—Skull and bones.
Sweater—Black V-neck sweater
or sweater vest (depending on
season).
Jacket—Scooter jacket. Black.
Socks—Two pairs.
T-shirts—Two fitted T's . . . yes,
black.
Underwear—Boxer briefs.
Passport.

Keep it simple and monochromatic
and you can go anywhere.
Hey, that might just be my new
philosophy. ◞

Don't miss the next
book by your favorite
author. Sign up now for
AuthorTracker by visiting
www.AuthorTracker.com.